Tinfoil Hats: Stories by Mad People in an Insane World

EDITED BY PHIL SMITH

Tinfoil Hats: Stories by Mad People in an Insane World.

Copyright 2023 Autonomous Press, LLC (Fort Worth, TX, 76114).

ISBN 978-1-945955-38-9
Ebook ISBN 978-1-945955-39-6

Edited by Phil Smith.

Cover art by Jacqueline Pruder St. Antoine. She's a multitalented creative bringing a mad studies perspective into new space. Her full bio is in the back of this book, but you can also visit her website at stantoineblog.wordpress.com

for m.
and for rilla, in my heart for almost a third of a century, and for all
of a life.

acknowledgements

editing a book means entering the lives of authors
here, authorities on and of their own lives.
their lives enter mine as editor, too.
this book wouldn't
have happened
without those
whose stories are told in these pages.

i've been influenced in weighs
that are hard to measure
by all the crazy people
that showed up in my life.
a couple are in this book.
one, dr. jacqueline pruder st. antoine
has taught me more about living Mad
with grace and class and joy
than anyone i know.
her writing, here and elsewhere
is sublime.

her art graces the cover
and makes the book
come alive.

there have been others—
importantly, rachel, kira, and lzz—
that continue to teach me about Madness.
there are more, too, that i won't name.

my colleagues and co-conspirators at autonomous press -
nick, andrew, martin, azzia, casandra, sean—
share their advice and counsel and experience and commitment
every day.
this thing wouldn't be here without them.

Table of Contents

tinfoil hats: stories by Mad people in an insane world— an introduction

PHIL SMITH

i'm Mad.
Mad as hell.
(not at you
at least not yet.)
crazy as a motherfucker, actually.
it's an identity i claim
from a re-claimed word
ripped up out of the cultural soil
 "...from its pejorative roots,
 drawing on the voices,
 knowledges,
 and perspectives

of self-identifying Mad persons..." (Castrodale, 2017, p. 60).
imma   lunatic
  loon   attic
  luna   tick
  loona swoona croona tiki tiki tavey.

i've been hanging around
Mad people my entire life
though they mostly didn't
or wouldn't lay claim to
that identity.
most would deny it, i think -
family members living
with depression (so much
depression
across so many generations
generational trauma, ya
know)
another traumatized by
growing up with an abu-
sive father

Madness is a "politicized identity" that "actively resists dominant discourses of 'mental illness,' reclaims language, and relates to ongoing social movements" (Reid, Snyder, Voronka, Landry, & Church, 2019). while lots of people "have been persuaded that many instances of unhappiness and discontent arise from biochemical abnormalities and require medical interventions... referred to as psychiatrization... we need to understand them as problems of communities or societies... consequences of the particular socio-economic conditions of late capitalism..." (Moncrieff, 2022, p. 2-3). and "Mad people see Madness not necessarily as a problem that needs treatment and but as a difference to be explored..." (Reid & Poole, 2013, p. 210)

a colleague whose arms were a quilt of burns and scars
a murdered uncle, a beloved weirdo aunt
and then more, and more
thrown into my life
or me into theirs
until i realized
these are my people
i'm one of them.
i'm one of us.

a coupla years ago
i began thinking about creating a collection
of stories and songs and poems (thanks, Utah)
written by people who identify as Mad.
i wanted to read their stories
asked them to describe
what it feels like
to live Mad in a saneist
world.
why?
or, maybe,
wry?
well, "Mental health
knowledge is dominated
by professional knowledge
to the exclusion of the
knowledge based on lived
experience (experiential
knowledge) that people
with mental health prob-
lems can bring" (Faulkner,
2017, p. 1).
because i take it for granted
that
"...insider and outsider
positions systematically
influence what kind of
knowledge is produced..."
(Stanley, 1993, p. 42),
i wanted to read stories

Sanism is "the systemic discrimination, the individualised prejudice, the structural barriers, as well as the fear, hatred, and distrust directed toward psychiatrised people" (LeFrançois, 2012, p. 7). Sanism is "an institutionalized, ideological process inherent in Western, Eurocentric, hegemonic culture founded in psychiatrism (the ideology of psychiatry) and the psy-complex (the set of practices, ideas, research, and social institutions that includes psychiatry, psychology, special education, social work, and other fields)" (Smith, 2020).

i reject the idea of mental health—i'm not sick or diseased. I've been Made Mad by the psy[spy] complex of linear, rational knowers—"...Madness has come to represent a critical alternative to 'mental illness' or 'disorder' as a way of naming and responding to emotional, spiritual, and neuro-diversity" (Menzies, LeFrançois, & Reaume, 2013, p. 10).

c/s/x/Mad (consumer/survivor/expatient/Mad people have been asking for a long time: "What and whose knowledge counts?" (Brosnan, 2018, p. 6)

that can't even be erased
because they never make it
on to the page. discounted
by definition
as knowers, our under-
standing of ourselves as
Mad people
is universally defined
by those who oppress us.
i   wanted—i   needed—to
hear Mad voices, part of a

"…little research space is provided to theories that challenge or conflict with the medical model. How, then, are service users to have their views and voices heard within this system and structure?" (Brosnan, 2018, p. 6)

"The psychiatrist said to us, point blank, "There is no point in asking them what they want, you know. They are all Mad. How are you going to get anything articulate out of this population?" (Cohen, 2022)

larger project of "…strategically reclaiming, contesting, and negotiating labels and treatments that are imposed on the Mad by psy sciences… Having a voice allows the Mad to construct counter-narratives… having a voice allows the Mad to challenge pervasive discourses of 'mental illness'" (Baylosis, 2019, p. 4).
i wanted to create the possibility of highlighting "…psychiatric survivor practices, Mad theorizings, and other forms of knowledge production emanating from Mad movements" (LeFrançois, Beresford, & Russo, 2016, p. 2), and to "…not only let Mad voices speak, but also opens up a space for these voices to articulate themselves on their own terms" (LeFrançois, Beresford, & Russo, 2016, p. 5)

so i asked a buncha
cray-cray people to   tell
            and   yell
            and   spell
            and   expel
            and   smell
            and   impel

　　　　and　　　　　　　　propel
their stow rees.
what i got was absolutely incredible
writ(h)ing
unhinged writing
about whirleds
unknown, unimagined
by all the normies.
it is work that is intensely personal
immensely difficult to write
immensely difficult to read
or talk
or think about.
they describe incidents and experiences
that are sometimes
shameful
horrifying
scary
hard.
also hilarious
joyful
spiritual
enlivening.
they put down in black ink
what it looks/feels/sounds/smells/tastes
like to be Made Mad
by people and systems and structures and ideologies
that stigmatize/psychiatrize/traumatize Mad people.

　i want to be clear:

this book was not conceived as

should not be read as

some kind of trauma porn

a way to get juiced

on the misery and distress of others.

nope.

nuttin like dat.

it is an intentionally and intensely

political project, a way to understand

Madness through the direct experience

of those who know-think-be-do it

every moment

of every hour

of every day

of every year

of their lives.

this book—these whirled word-worlds -

exist because

Mad people have

real knowledge

real understanding

real lives

worthy of being shared.

it is also a way to take a stand, because

"self-identifying Mad persons are engaged in ongoing epistemic border policing to secure ideological territory and prevent the co-option and collusion of Mad perspectives by countering non-Mad sanist sentimentalities..." (Castrodale, 2017, p. 52).

Mad people have been

    talked about

described
inscribed
diagnosed
controlled
by people from the privileged

    psy-   complex
    spy-   complex
for much too long.
their own stories have been
denied and co-opted.
it's time to take those stories back.
it's time to reclaim our
identities.
that's what this book is
about.
taking back what we never gave away.

the psy complex is made up of a number of biomedically based disciplines that include "...psychiatry but also... psychology, nursing, and social work. Together these and other allied professions form what is known as the *psy complex,* which is an expansive and overarching system that informs and intersects with other neoliberal systems of oppression..." (LeFrançois, Beresford, & Russo, 2016, p. 5)

for too long
even when
stories by Mad people
have been heard out
they have been coopted
by the psy-complex
and others in places
of power and control
to serve their own needs.
here, i seek to avoid that cooption
understanding that once
they get out in the world

i won't be able to control them.
with others (Voronka, 2019),
i trouble ways in which these stories
are heard and understood
through the bodyminds of
the psy-industrial complex
and the dominating, epistemic,
neoliberal, hegemonic,
people-killing onto-epistemologies
they co/re-create.
the stories here, and the bodyminds
they reflect, speak against
the psy-spys and all they represent.
they are not inrecovery.
they are not resilient.
they stand opposed to simplistic
understandings of mental health (Voronka, 2019).
they are politically opposed to all dat
reflected in their insistence of
and identity as actual Mad people.

still, i understand and believe in
the power
"of storytelling to challenge biomedical ideologies
and oppressive power structures" (O'Donnell, Sapouna, & Brosnan, 2019, p. 2).
i believe that
"they allow us to challenge bio-psychiatry
and dominant understandings of human distress
and to create alternative views;

most importantly,
they connect us with each other
as we find we are not alone.
This is the most significant potential
of narrating our experiences;
it builds community
and allows a politicised, collective consciousness
to emerge among psychiatrised people" (O'Donnell, Sapouna, &
Brosnan, 2019, p. 9).

Mad   studies
Mad   activism
Mad   people
are in a big tent.
they are   diverse
they are   divergent
in ways beyond   neurodivergence
                              neurodiversity.
they believe in different things
think differently
arrive at different conclusions
have differing politics and ideas.
but it seems to me that they share
one thing in common:
they "oppose the illness model of mental difference and the hege-
mony of psychiatry" (Brewer, 2018, p. 14).

i have become convinced that
"Madness is a way of knowing…" (Cooper, 1978, p. 155).
speaking of his own Madness playing out as depression

Castrodale describes it
   "as representing a rich critical interpretive
      lens, where depressive feelings guide
      knowledge and provide access to truths" (2017, p. 51).
these truths may not be those of others
but they are ours
as real and valid and true as
any of those around us.
they offer insight and inspiration
about the whirleds and the whorleds and the peoples.
it belongs to all the beings:
"Madness is a common social property
   that has been stolen from us,
like the reality of our dreams
and our deaths:
we have to get these things back politically
so that they become creativity and spontaneity
in a transformed society" (Cooper, 1978, p. 14).
this book is a step toward taking them back.

it has become
common-place
in some circles
to offer a content warning—
a signal to readers
who might be triggered
by some kinds
of meanings and knowledge and
stories and experiences
that are just too close to home.

summa da in[out]divided-dual{single} auteurs
of these chap tours have offered up
content warnings for their writhings here
which got me thinkervating:
this whole dang book needs a content   war   ning
                                                   peace
                                                   light   ning   bolt
                                                   nuts and

so here tis: consider yourself   (deprecating)
                                   (defecating)
                                   (urinating)
                        warned
                        warmed:
there is much here that may be troubling to and for and by
those who   have been and
          will be   traumatterized
                    cauterized
                    samsonized
by peoples who seek to cause harm
(and be aware that trauma is caused by   real people
                        people with names and addresses
                        and their own traumas.
be careful out there.

   jenn layton annabelle is an autistic, Mad parent to a newborn human, who describes their experience at the hands of professionals unable to understand the experience of being an autistic parent in their chapter "Bleeding insanity: one person's story of Madness, menstruation, and Neurodivergence." they are institutionalised after giving birth, "judged silently," as they say in their chapter, "by professionals acting as judge, jury, and executioner," and then again, in a "crisis house," from which friends helped them escape.

jersey consantino constructs a Mad and Trans poesis in their chapter "chartering (un)knowability: Mapping Transness and Madness within the interstices of becoming." they describe falling asleep (sort of), listening as a peer support volunteer, coming out—memories and birthdays and thoughts and dreams and television and voices and interstices and and and and and too much too little all at once.

in their chapter "coming out twice: how my 'nuclear meltdown' helped me embrace my Madness and autism," Australian professor of politics and international relations benjamin habib describes a television interview that goes awry, resulting in their accepting and then publicly claiming identities of Madness and Autism. they explore how these intersecting identities have affected their life, and the social masks that they adopted to disguise their anxiety and social awkwardness.

leah heilig and bailey kirby write about the lighter and darker side of Madness in their chapter "killing the mood: a bi-vocal commentary on bipolar humor," in which they tell a series of "somewhat fractured and fucked-up" series of stories in which their "experiences of mania, depression, and mixed cycles" lurch through and around into what they acknowledge are "a bunch of uncomfortable jokes." if they don't make ya laugh, I dunno what will.

monica shield's chapter, "a perfect graveyard of buried hopes," describes what it's like after waking up from having mysteriously spent forty years in the Puerto Rican jungle, only to be brought to hospital, against their will, for reasons that aren't clear, and forcibly medicated. they manage to escape, in rather desperate circumstances, and slowly re-enter a world that no longer makes particular sense. dark, confusing, deprived of human connection: life as a mad person.

in "hello satan," helen silverwood's protagonist moves out of a psychiatric hospital and into a hostel, the head of which, mr. casey, is a man with hair "the shade of dead cod that had been slowly stewed in a puddle of dirty water"—that phrase may give you an idea of the kind of wonderful writing you'll find here. after looking at him carefully for some weeks (with an unnerving autistic gaze), the story's protagonist realizes that mr. casey is, in fact, the actual satan, out to steal the souls of unsuspecting residents. they devise a plan to eliminate mr. casey and—well, you'll have to read the rest of the story to see how it turns out.

"weighting/the machine: whut Mad[ness] is Mad[e] uv" explores Madness through divergent poetry. ranging across systemic analytics of the psy/spy complex, through short narratives of trauma, to quotes about the rootedness of Madness in western culture, it/they unpacks sanism through the eyes of a recovering university professor.

jacquie pruder st. antoine describes their existence, alongside a cat named pigeon, in a small apartment-cum-purgatory, where they are kept safe by purple sweaters and green coats, throwing dishes instead of washing them, the line that "separates a bird-human-woman-bodymind from the human-people who walk in their human-suits", in a piece titled "cat-pigeon and bird-woman."

"charleston memorial," by aubry threlkeld, describes growing up in southeast united states, in a series of vignettes that are filled with trauma after trauma after trauma. suicide, domestic violence, murder, generations of rape—the thought that a single young person might experience all of this in one lifetime is truly difficult to comprehend. the chapter weaves and wanders through time and space, memory and reality, near and far.

devin turk's short chapter, "Mad out loud," describes in broad brush their life as a Mad, autistic, neuroqueer, trans person, commenting on identity, language, and a lifetime of being a person in the psychiatric system. they describe what it means "...to be *Mad out loud*. To be Mad out loud means I must work in the direction of a Mad identity that is political in addition to deeply personal. It means listening to my intuition, and it means valuing the sound of my own voice even when it speaks alone."

these stories
all written by neurodivergent people
who identify as being Mad
are about living Mad in a saneist world.
they are intensely personal
as intensely as can be done
when the intensity is difficult
to write or talk about.
they include stories
about incidents and experiences
that are intensely shameful
horrifying
scary
hard.
they are narratives
about what it looks

feels

sounds

smells

tastes

like to be Mad

experiences of interacting

with those who stigmatize

psychiatrize

traumatize

Mad people.

read on.

this is the real deal.

this is us.

REEFER SENSES

Baylosis, C. (2019). Mad studies and an ethics of listening. *Journal of Ethics in Mental Health, 10,* 1-18.

Brewer, E. (2018). Coming out Mad, coming out disabled. In E. J. Donaldson (ed.), *Literatures of Madness*. Palgrave. doi: 10.1007/978-3-319-92666-7_2

Brosnan, L. (2018). Who's talking about us without us? A survivor research interjection into an academic psychiatry debate on compulsory community treatment orders in Ireland. *Laws,* 7(33). doi:10.3390/laws7040033

Castrodale, M. (2017).Critical disability studies and Mad studies: Enabling new pedagogies in practice.

The Canadian Journal for the Study of Adult Education, 29(1) 49–66.

Cohen, B. (2022, May 25). The failings of "mental health": How a seemingly benign concept might be dangerous (Interview by Ayurdhi Dhar). *Mad in America.* https://www.madinamerica.com/2022/05/failings-mental-health-dangerous/

Cooper, D. (1978). *The language of Madness.* Penguin Books.

Faulkner, A. (2017).Survivor research and Mad Studies: The role and value of experiential knowledge in mental health research *Disability & Society,* 1-21. doi: 10.1080/09687599.2017.1302320

LeFrançois, B., Beresford, P., Russo, J. (2016). Editorial: Destination Mad Studies. *Intersectionalities: A Global Journal of Social Work Analysis, Research, Polity, and Practice, 5*(3), 1-10.

Menzies, R., LeFrançois, B., & Reaume, G. (2013). Introducing Mad studies. In B. LeFrançois, R. Menzies, & G. Reaume (Eds.) *Mad matters: A critical reader in Canadian Mad studies* (pp. 1-22). Toronto, Canada: Canadian Scholars Press, Inc.

Moncrieff, J. (2022). The political economy of the mental health system: A Marxist analysis. *Frontiers in Sociology, 6,* 1-11. doi: 10.3389/fsoc2021.771875

O'Donnell, A., Sapouna, L., and Brosnan, L. (2019). Storytelling: An act of resistance or a commodity? *Journal of Ethics in Mental Health, 10,* 1-13.

Reid, J., Snyder, S., Voronka, J., Landry, D., and Church, K. (2019). Mobilizing Mad art in the neoliberal university: Resisting regulatory efforts by inscribing art as political practice. *Journal of Literary & Cultural Disability Studies, 13*(3) 255-271. doi:10.3828/jlcds.2019.20

Reid, J. & Poole, J. (2013). Mad students in the social work classroom? Notes from the beginnings of an inquiry. *Journal of Progressive Human Services,* 24:209–222. doi: 10.1080/10428232.2013.835185

Smith, P. (2020). (R)evolving towards Mad: Spinning away from the psy/spy-complex through auto/biography. In J. Parsons & A. Chappell (Eds.) *The Palgrave handbook of auto/biography* (pp. 369-388). Palgrave Macmillan. doi: 10.1007/978-3-030-31974-8_16

Stanley, L. (1993). On auto/biography in sociology. *Sociology, 27*(1), 41-52.Voronka, J. (2019). Storytelling beyond the psychiatric gaze: Resisting resilience and recovery narratives. *Canadian Journal of Disability Studies, 8*(4).

bleeding insanity: one person's story of Madness, menstruation, and Neurodivergence

JENN LAYTON ANNABLE

Blood; bled; bleeding; to bleed. The red flower blossoming on the gusset of my pants surprised me and the coppery tang of blood assailed my brain. I was ten and I had just started my period. The first defining moment of my life had come to pass. I was now a woman in a child's body, upon whose head a culture organised and constructed by men was about to bestow a whole history of gender-based expectations, violence, and inequality. God help me. This is the story I hope to share with you, one of bleeding insanity: of Madness, menstruation, and neurodivergence.

·

I am Jenn.

I am of a physical body which evolved biologically to create, grow, and feed another human organism, and which is often perceived as female. The consciousness and experience living inside this tissue mass is different though. It doesn't really know what it is yet, because the words to describe it sufficiently do not yet exist.

Like millions of people before me, I've experienced madness, inextricably interwoven with my perceived femaleness and intensified by my neurodivergence. My insanity, caused by my menstrual cycle, my sensitivity to the hormones that course through me each month, made things this way for me.

I am described...

...as living with autism, which is a professional term derived from non-autistic people's perceptions of me/us, but which is the only thing until recently that I and those with similar differences had to collectively identify ourselves with.

Neurodivergent is better. Useful, as it is something we have constructed to describe ourselves. It allows us to stand collectively and commune with a diversity of other neurotypes, for us to recognise each other, exclaiming "I am...," "We are...," At the moment though, it is still too broad for me to specifically understand myself through when I am searching for the meaning in my unique experience. *"I am autistic"* is the peace I have made with myself between these points. This is adequate for the moment.

...as a woman, which I'm simply not. The gender in my head, the expression of what I am to myself, bears no resemblance to the breasts and vulva I embody physically. I am male on some days, female on others and on the rest I'm not quite sure. I am fluid, a molten instability of stuff, which is the way I like it. Why would being fixed be better? Life is always moving and surging forwards, is it not?

Isn't it interesting how being fixed is described as both being static or constant, at the same time as being made well, describing how one might improve upon undesirable damage?

Many people have tried to fix me in both ways. None have succeeded, thank the Goddesses.

I am Mad; identified that is. I reject the medicalised notions of mental disorder that have been inflicted upon me by researchers, doctors, and healthcare professionals. My Madness is a part of me, like being autistic is. Being Mad has raised me to the light and plunged me into the darkness, which have all contributed to the 'I' that sits here writing these words. Both have taught me about myself.

My trouble begins when I intersect with the dominant neurotypical culture and society in which I live. It has very different ideas, about gender, neurotypes, and sanity, which I sadly fail to embody. It is not enough for me to be happy and well. I have to conform, obey, and mask, too. Any need or desire to deviate is met with stigma, humiliation, and correction, which devastated me and the sense of who and what I am for a long time.

I am hysterical. I am unworthy. I am perceived as woman, bleeding, and worst of all, different.

•

Boom. Boom. Boom. Boom.

The blood in my ears sounds like the heavy march of soldiers surging tirelessly forward towards dawn carrying my insomnia on their shoulders. Another night without sleep; so, so tired.

This is the pain of menstruation, the agony of my body.

Vomiting. Shitting. A stomach distended with water retention and alcohol drunk to take the edge off the knife which slowly peels away my skin in my monthly death by one thousand cuts. Cramps so bad it feels like someone is winding your insides out, twisting them slowly around themselves until you want to scream in agony.

But you can't.

You have to smile. You have to nod. Turn up to work looking presentable, hiding the dark shadows beneath your eyes with make up. Paint yourself female, even if you don't recognise what you see in the mirror as that. You don't even know the person who looks back at you, you're hiding so far away behind the mask you wear for the world. This is the burden of being a woman, a heavy load intensified many times when you are also autistic, hiding your Mad and your differences with you in your dark.

Smell intense. Sounds unbearable. Sight and light blinding. So usually bad, so much worse when the blood comes. Feeling like you just want to die every moment and not really knowing how to get through the minutes, but somehow managing to in spite of yourself.

Every month. Every month. Every month. This was menstruation before the madness came.

When I had birthed my boy, fed him for eleven months and started to feel better, the blood came back, unexpected after I had been lulled into a false sense of security.

Blood again. Red for danger. Red for death. Red for plague, a bright slash across my underwear warning me to run away from the thing dripping out of me. A red flag waved to warn of impending danger. Only I didn't know it as that, because I didn't know how bad it was going to get this time.

How are you supposed to run away from yourself?

Anger is described as a red mist. Only this feeling, this sensation that descended with the red from the slash between my legs felt like drowning in a sea of gore, the upward spray of an artery as the knife cuts deep, filling your head with hatred, anger, and out of control, so out of control.

This feeling was new and unknown, much worse than before birth.

The beat came back. The blood beat, the heart beat. The out of control beat, rising higher and faster and faster and higher until all I had was the capacity left to scream in rage like a beast, scream like the injured elephant protecting its calf as the hunters circle.

That's all I wanted to do. Protect my baby. Live a quiet life, away from the noise and the panic and the chaos. But my baby became all these things. A loved and hated being that became the glowing centre of my world, an ember of life burning so bright. He erupted cries that made us both panic and left me gasping for breath.

Keep it in. Keep it in. Keep it in. My new mantra.

•

I did not identify as autistic or neurodivergent until over twenty years after my period started. The period (always periods) in between contained much haemoglobin. I self harmed by cutting; my nose bled when I took too many drugs; coagulating into bruises from being assaulted by a violent partner; birthing the joy that is my son for over forty hours. Blood on his head like a primal baptism, holding him, still unaware of the overwhelming flood of confusion and misery that was about to erupt over the landscape of our happiness only weeks later.

Although I had struggled with living and being in the world, I had always coped well enough to pass undetected from the superintendents of social normativity in the mental health neglect system. I cut where I could hide the scars, earned enough money to cover my coke habit, was always straight enough to turn up and perform my job to the expected level.

Having a child had long been a dream of mine I believed impossible to fulfil. When I was progressing slowly through the agony of puberty I didn't understand why people wanted to reproduce—what was the point of bringing more fucked up people into the world—weren't there enough of us already? By age thirty though, I had achieved a modicum of professional success and met someone I loved. My hope was rekindled and we desired to have a child.

This baby, this second defining moment of my life, combined the two inescapable facts about myself that became irreversible when he was born: I was autistic (I just didn't know it yet); I was a parent. They conspired to erase the identity I had constructed to that point. Madness prevailed, quite literally.

I was admitted to a specialist Mother and Baby Psychiatric Unit in the United Kingdom in December 2012. My child was not quite five months old. For the previous five weeks I had been experiencing violent and traumatising mental images that included me hanging myself, drowning both me and my child; seeing the blood stream from the slashes I made in my arms, piles of tidy clothes left in a pram next to a lakeside, or my partner finding my swinging body suspended from the ceiling. I was suicidal, exhausted, and unable to even string two words together most of the time.

The doctors and nurses seemed kind. "Come and stay for a few days", they said. "Take a break from your stresses at home" (we had moved house with a three month old into a property that required major renovation). To my exhausted bodymind, the inpatient facility seemed like some hotel with the added bonus of diazepam and nursery-nurse support if you needed to sleep. I knew that my capacity to care for myself and my son was reducing every day. I was so grateful for the chance to just get some rest and find out why I was struggling so much compared to the other parents.

Unfortunately, like many other times between that day and this, I was about to collide with a very different reality.

I had always been proud of the fact that I researched the choices I made and backed them up with facts. The difference between my ideas and those of the staff in the unit about parenting soon brought us into conflict though. My co-sleeping was described as dangerous and I was forbidden from doing it, despite the fact this was how we had slept since birth. The difficulties I had with staff entering my room each hour and shining a torch over me to check I was still present were dismissed as being awkward. In reality I was being woken up each night by the light because of my sensory sensitivities, as well as breastfeeding, and then castigated for not getting up and dressed promptly each morning.

Activities I had typically done to meet my sensory needs, such as hula-hooping whilst watching television, were pathologised. My partner was called in and questioned about this when staff encountered it, the query phrased to him as whether this was "normal" for me. I was even shamed by senior nurses for wearing shorts and t-shirt (after being told to treat the space like home) because there were men around on the ward.

The staff were judgmental, narrow-minded, and fixed in their thinking. I quickly grew to dislike and then hate spending time there. I tried to leave one weekend. I was told that I would be placed under a Section (an involuntary detention people believed to be a danger to themselves are subject to in the UK, named after a 'Section' of the Mental Health Act that grants this power to clinicians) if I walked out before the consultant psychiatrist spoke to me the following week. This was, I discovered later, an unlawful assertion, but one which took advantage of my vulnerability and ignorance, as so often happens with autistic people.

So I stayed.

One sliver of hope remained for me, beyond just getting out of the madhouse I had admitted myself into with as much sanity as I came in with—finally getting an answer to the questions I had about my differences and difficulties I had prior to becoming pregnant.

Would I finally get the answer I had been pursuing for the last ten years?

•

My madness had crept in surreptitiously whilst my child grew. My son expanded in my belly, slowly taking up room used for other things: an act of creation celebrating love.

The madness expanded in my mind at the same pace, also taking up room used for other things, slowly, slowly, imperceptibly. The outline of it was there all along, like that of a tiny hand or foot through the skin of your body, but unnoticed because it was unexpected.

What I now know to be its shape was already present before I birthed. The euphoria and high of mania was mistaken for the joy of expecting my son. My energy and restlessness put down to 'nesting'. I was the author of my own self delusion. I am fine. Everything is fine. Everything will be fine when I give birth. Ev-

erything will be fine when he starts to sleep through the night…
Everything…

Only it wasn't.

Within weeks of meeting my baby, my life was collapsing. I couldn't eat, couldn't sleep, couldn't cope with the simplest things that had been effortless before. I became wracked with anxieties. The life I now led, just me and my baby, caused the structure and routine I had relied upon all my life as an unidentified autistic person who needed context, to disappear.

I know now that the problem was that I have no sense of interoception. I cannot tell when I am hungry, or thirsty, unless these sensations are so overwhelming that they eclipse everything else. The trouble was that by the time I realised what I needed I was too exhausted to do anything about it and instead fell asleep starving. My sensory perceptions, exquisitely responsive, became a red hot scalpel poking my brain—the crying, the smells of baby puke and shit, sour milk, hands on my breasts, my breasts themselves full, leaking, squirting milk, making me feel like a fucking cow. Everything I experienced just hurt.

I stumbled through the first four months of motherhood, a sense of weight growing about me. The noise of my son crying made me want to throw him across the room sometimes. I hated trying to get to sleep, which I could not do. I hated the arrival of dawn which meant I had to get up and begin again, which was increasingly beyond me. I tried and I failed. I hated myself for it, for not being able to do all the other things everyone around me seemed to achieve so effortlessly. The story of my life.

The lack of any self identity I now experienced externally (mummy, not Jenn) reflected the void in my mind, in my being, the emptiness where before there was meaning and purpose. The special interests that had sustained and defined me before my son was born were now unavailable. I was mother and didn't have time or right to these anymore.

I talked to people, the professionals, midwives, health visitors (nurses who support new mothers in the UK). I tried to explain to them. I didn't have the words though. Words they would have understood. Words that I needed to know to understand myself and the mountain I was climbing on my own with my baby on my back, a whole world of ignorance dragging behind me, holding me back.

Instead I masked (a learned behaviour associated with autistic people, in which they learn to perform in socially acceptable ways to pass undetected by the neurotypical majority). This was taken at face value, with nobody probing deeper than a tired mother who was experiencing the 'baby blues'. This primary coping mechanism as an uncomprehended neurodivergent became my undoing. I continued to maintain the front that had held in a lifetime of grief, anguish and self doubt, whilst holding strong against the world outside. This edifice of self, which has been constructed brick by painful brick from mistakes I made together with abuse and humiliation I was subject to, crumbled under the tsunami of distress that the combination of being autistic, perceived as female, and a parent unleashed.

What I have described here, what it was like for me, being autistic whilst not knowing, was like living in a hell personally designed to exact a punishment for something that is so terrible I could not comprehend it. I knew what was expected of me, understood what I had to do, yet consistently failed. I could see everyone around me doing it. I tried, and tried and tried, as hard as I could. To be a good person. To not be fussy, arrogant, difficult, angry or a problem. I failed though, all the time, every time. I never, ever won.

This becomes the lens through which I experienced the world and my place in it.

This sense of failure has been so bad in my life that I have cut and harmed myself countless times. I have tried to commit suicide twice because of it.

I am so thankful I did not succeed though. I have so much to live for.

•

Bloodshed. These wounds inflicted upon female perceived autistic persons are hidden, just like our disabilities. Just like us.

In the Mother and Baby Unit, the neurotypical smiles and assurances that everything was fine was hiding a growing sub-narrative of perceived problems about how I was looking after my son, responding to him, caring for him.

This was all communicated through the unspoken language of the body, the facial expression, the tone of voice. I didn't stand a chance of addressing it because I didn't perceive it. My value as a parent, as a responsible human being, was judged silently by professionals acting as judge, jury, and executioner.

In the end I received a referral to Children's Social Services identifying my son as being at potential risk of harm from me. I knew this wasn't true. I had to do something to defend myself—but where on earth to begin?

Me, one Mad mother, with a six month old baby, recently released from an inpatient psychiatric facility, was taking on the resident Consultant Psychiatrist who had returned from leave and declared I was not autistic, blocking my referral for a diagnostic assessment in the process, along with her team of "expert" professionals whose speciality was mentally ill mothers, and their babies.

I knew I was going to be in for the fight of my life. I didn't realise it was the beginning of THE long fight for my life, my identity and my rights, that began when I chose to stop being invisible. I knew I was autistic whatever anyone else said. I just had to make other people see it, and me too.

This was the choice I made and continue to make. It is a hard choice, but the right one.

•

At the beginning of this process my data became my armour.

In the UK, citizens have rights in law to access or obtain a copy of the personal information held about them by an organisation. I applied for and received, from the hospital that treated me, a body of paper documents over four inches thick which consisted of all my notes, records, and clinical observations, amalgamated from my time as both an inpatient and outpatient at the Mother and Baby Unit.

I reviewed everything. Nurse reported scales assessing how I interacted with my baby, pharmaceutical notes, clinical risk assessments, and ward observations. To truly understand the contents, I had to comprehend what the document was, how it was compiled, what the information contained in it was, and how it would be likely to be interpreted by a professional reading it.

The comments here made me cry, when I truly understood how my actions and motivation had been interpreted and recorded by professionals for professionals to read, with no opportunity for me to contribute to or challenge them.

Excerpts from my notes:

"Eye contact breaks are longer and mother seems to initiate eye contact less often, giving the impression that she is too distractible to do so" [the underlining was the clinician's].

"Been walking around the unit in underwear (shorts and vest), quite revealing—advised to put more clothes on and that there was a male visiting the ward... doesn't acknowledge this as inappropriate."

They held the power. To define me. To label me. To pathologise me.

I needed to gain command over my own story.

Gradually, over a period of weeks and months, I stitched together a suit of scales. Each one was a tiny facet of fact from my personal data. It transformed into a glittering costume, illuminating every issue I wished to raise about my experience as a patient and the judgement I had been subject to by those paid and trained to support me. I was clothed beautifully in this, adorning myself in the evidence from professionals' own records, making my complaints irrefutable.

This narrative, once constructed, became my sword and shield. I had been discounted, humiliated, denied, and ignored. The sense of fury that filled me became the means through which I battled not only to clear my name as a mother, but also to clear my head. I gained a sense of purpose to fight the fear, the sense of failure that pervaded my daily experience.

In working with, then through this anger. It and I transformed. We became something new, something joined that was greater in our synergy, better than either could be on its own.

I don't know what this thing is, but like my madness from before, I was able to feel the shape of it, trace the line of its power. It runs both within me, through the threads of this story that I am telling today that has in turn become my history, which has joined with those of the millions of other menstruating, neurodivergent people who have been discounted, locked away and denied for so long.

•

I received an "official" diagnosis of "high-functioning autism" from a clinician in March 2015, after waiting nearly three years after my discharge as an inpatient. The team that undertook this were excellent; knowledgeable, supportive, insightful. This act of diagnosis was my third defining moment.

I was still left with mixed feelings.

I thought I had, in the time I had spent awaiting the chance for a professional with a manual to confirm what I already knew, come to terms with what being autistic was, and meant, for me and my family.

Looking back, I experienced this period of my life as a burning, an inferno that reached the stars in my sky, obliterating the view of my future from my eyes. Everything that I had, everything that I hoped for, everything that I was, became lost in a bonfire of my dreams. It extinguished every hope that I had of being able to live a normal life: return to work, study for higher qualifications, parent my child on my own, be a partner to his father again.

The pain I experienced made the past agony of menses and childbirth fall away into insignificance.

Unpicking the threads of cause and effect took me years. Although I had believed I was autistic, receiving the diagnosis fell like a hammer blow. My distress intensified, I ended up being hospitalised twice more in 2015.

Yet, still within all this, I found in hospital with other mad people that there was the calm centre of this storm that raged around and inside me. I discovered whilst an inpatient this time the joy, humility, and candour of people who live with mental distress in their daily existence. I began to realise that life was possible. Fun was possible. That professionals were entitled to disapprove when I made tinfoil helmets with erect penis embellishments, but that I didn't have to care about this. I was my own person, professionals did not have the answer or the question. They did not control me, or how I felt about myself... that if I was going to reclaim my dreams, my identity, I had to do it on my own terms.

I was my recovery, no more no less. I was my autistic, no more no less. I was my Madness, no more no less. I was my wonderful, no more no less.

My ultimate turning point to recovery and where I find myself today happened at the beginning of 2017. Things had settled. I was more stable. I had a social worker (who was and still is amazing, thank you Beth) and a community psychiatric nurse who were both supportive. I had commenced a course of therapy which I reacted very badly to. To support me, I was admitted to a Crisis House, a community-located recovery setting that supported people to avoid hospital. Despite it being run by a charity organisation, places were still commissioned by the public healthcare sector. The Crisis Team, mental health nurses and doctors supposed to be providing intensive support, were gatekeepers to the places.

I spent two weeks in the Crisis House. On the last weekend had a particularly severe meltdown. I was coping really badly, terrified of going home as I was going to be on my own for three days before my partner returned from work, contending with increasingly strong urges to hurt myself.

The non-clinical crisis house staff (who were wonderful) were happy for me to stay with them until my partner came back; no other referrals had been made. The room would be empty. The crisis team staff were resolute. They were not prepared to allow me to stay under any circumstances. I responded by saying I would refuse to leave and lock myself in my room. I was told that the crisis house staff had been instructed by the crisis team nurses to call the police and have them physically remove me if I did this.

I simply could not comprehend this. It went beyond my understanding of how a person feeling as I did could be disregarded, treated like an animal. The only reaction I had left was to bang my head against a brick wall until I had mashed the hair, skin and scalp there into a bloodied mess, screaming all the time. I was physically restrained, then taken to the emergency room with suspected concussion and neck injuries.

Do you remember that hell I described earlier? The personal hell I described, in which I tried as hard as I could but in which I always failed?

As I lay on the bed in the emergency room cubicle I contemplated my life and what I hoped to do with it. The past year things seemed to have been improving, however like always it was snatched away. I was reduced again to behaving like an animal, being treated like an animal, seeing that red spray of anger, and knowing what was coming, and that there was nothing at all I could do to stop it. This was the deepest pain of this hell. It convinced you again and again that this time it was all going to work out okay.

I was done with believing these lies.

I decided that I didn't want to live like this. I didn't want to put my son or family through this pain with me anymore. I closed my eyes and made my plans. I would leave the hospital through a side entrance, walk to a local bar and borrow a phone, saying my car had broken down, and that I needed a taxi. I would return to the crisis house, obtain all the prescribed diazepam/valium that I had there, which was a lot (support staff were not able to refuse me this because they were not healthcare qualified). I would get my car, go home, stopping to buy alcohol and paracetamol on my way back. Once there I would lock and barricade all downstairs doors, remove and destroy the phone, and take everything I had. I didn't wish to be dissuaded, I just wanted to be left alone to die in peace.

This was the most complete and detailed suicide plan I had ever made. Most importantly, the inner turmoil that had always convulsed within me was silent. After five years of not knowing what to do for the best, I knew that ending my life was the right decision. That my partner, our son, and this world would definitely be a better place for my absence. My son could get on with his life with his sane parent who has supported us both through so many cycles of madness and bleeding.

I had stopped fighting myself. The pain had ended. I intended to follow it.

Keeping an eye on the nursing staff, I pulled the curtain across a little more and gingerly tried walking. I left the emergency room unchallenged, executing all the steps of my plan right up to when I went to collect my medication from the crisis house staff. This was the point at which my life was saved, quite literally.

I was informed by the support worker on duty that my friends (who I spoke to earlier that day) had been so concerned about my safety that they had driven three hours without my knowledge to come and collect me and take me home.

I stopped and took stock. I do not believe in divine intervention, but this is the closest experience I have had in my life to something that might be described in this way. It felt like the universe wanted to send me the clearest message that it could—that I was wanted, that people who cared for and loved me would be there when I needed them.

I decided to wait and see.

Even though I am not in touch with any of the people that supported me over that weekend and kept me safe until my partner got home, I will forever be grateful to them all. They saved my life, and kept me safe. After returning home I woke up with abdominal pain, blood on the sheets. It transpired that the whole episode I had been experiencing was because I had missed enough of the medication I used to suppress ovulation for it to become ineffective. The stress of the therapy made me forget to take it—such a simple mistake to make.

The fact was though, that of all the mental health doctors, nurses, therapists, and other specialists who I came into contact with over the previous three weeks, none of them had spotted what the real problem was. I was bleeding again. It was my period. Nothing more, nothing less. It was documented, written up, and available information, if someone had just dug a little deeper. Instead I was filled up to the brim with addictive drugs, provoked, traumatised and restrained, then finally threatened with eviction from a place of safety when I protested.

My friends and I kept me safe. We figured out what the issue was, then put in place the mechanisms that stopped me from hurting myself, or worse. Company, joy, small reminders of my humanity, and what I had to live for was all I needed.

This is what I have been doing every day since. I'm also now doing it for my son who is in danger of being equally badly shafted by health, education, and welfare systems that ignore neurodivergent people. Trying to avoid the damage of drug abuse, sexual exploitation, self harm, and suicidality being inflicted on his head. Experiences I would not wish on my worst enemy, and unthinkable in all his innocence and joy.

The attempts by professionals to narrate me on my behalf continues unabated.

Now I am controlling, manipulative, and inflexible (er, autistic?). I have the audacity to "complain when I don't get the support I want" (read entitled to by law in the UK). Unfortunately for those same individuals doing my narrating for me, and luckily for me, I have a very firm grasp on what I need to thrive and the privilege of education, language, and experience to make my case in a way that is very difficult to refute. I get very angry when 'experts-by-qualification' are paid an awful lot of money to not do the job they are employed for. I'm not well liked in some quarters. I know I have made, and am making, a positive difference to an equal degree in just as many others as well.

This is the choice I am able to make. I also appreciate that there are so many other female perceived autistic persons and other neurodivergent persons, disabled persons, just persons, who are not lucky enough to have the advantages I enjoy, to do the same.

I don't know how to make the world right for all of us, but I am trying as hard as I can.

I am trying to cultivate a little corner of it in the right way. Make sure my neurodivergent son grows up with a vocabulary that he chooses, which describes his strengths and attributes accurately. Friends like him; people like us. A community of diverse positive role models that incorporate the many body types, neurotypes, and identities that he might one day choose for himself, but ultimately through which he understands that it's okay to be different. That being so can be a strength, a new way of looking at the world that has already silently contributed so much to human history.

I am trying to learn. Not to judge others in the way I have been judged. I have been guilty of this without even realising. To live in the moment, always experiencing the beauty of it, even if it is fleeting or hard to grasp. There is much beauty in this, my story, alongside the blood and pain. There is love, life, light, and Madness. Where would we be without Madness?

I hope that in reading my story, whoever, wherever, and whenever you are, we have been able to connect in a way that has been meaningful to you. I wish you well whatever your challenges. I stand by you in identity, Madness, and blood, whatever those signify for you and your life.

I see you. You see me.

We see.

We.

20th February 2021.

chartering (un)knowability: mapping Transness and Madness within the interstices of becoming

JERSEY COSANTINO

Acknowledgments

This chapter and my exploration of a Mad and trans poesis would not be possible without the unwavering support, compassion, and care of my academic advisor, Dr. Mike Gill, Associate Professor of Disability Studies in the department of Cultural Foundations of Education at Syracuse University. It is a direct result of his transformative teaching and mentorship that I have found a home within Mad and trans scholarship and, for this, I will be forever grateful.

Out
I came out as gay at 19,
queer at 21,
genderqueer at 22,
nonbinary at 30,
trans at 31
and Mad at 33,
coming out experiences
that were inextricably intertwined
and made possible
by coming out
stories that came before,
and coming out stories that
inevitably
will come after.
Each time that I come out
and navigate the people, places,
and spaces
where this disclosure
is needed,
desired,
and undesired,
I expel a half-hearted
sigh of relief
knowing that the burden
of holding a part of me
that has so *long*ed to be acknowledged,
heard,
and understood,
is finally being released,

finding expression both within myself
and outside of
myself,
claiming a truth
that I had previously *refused* to believe
and genuinely
and truly
see[1]...

The first step to seeing is seeing that there are things you do not see, it said.

...I don't understand.

The creature sighed...If you do not know there are things you do not see, it said, then you will not see them because you do not expect them to be there. You think you see everything, so you think everything you see is all there is to be seen.

So, there are things hiding?...

There is the unseen, waiting to be seen, existing only in the spaces we admit we do not see *yet*. [emphasis added] (Emezi, 2019, pp. 71-72)

Yet
At the end of each coming out story,
(right when there should be a period,
a hard stop to a declamatory statement
that has waited a lifetime to be affirmed,

but, for some disturbing reason,
always feels residually interrogative),
as soon as the weight begins to lift
and air starts to fill my chest
once more,
I can feel this tightness,
this troubling foreboding,
emerging from within,
swirling around my organs,
entangling my heart,
restricting my lungs,
and gripping progressively
tighter around my jaw,
neck, and shoulders.
Creeping closer and closer,
until it knows
that I cannot look away,
cannot run away,
cannot ignore it
any longer,
I swear
I can make out a whisper
that says,
that conjures:

Don't forget,
"[w]hat we 'look for'
is un/fortunately what
we shall find" (Minh-ha, 1989, p. 141),
and

you,
you,
you,
have woefully,
naively,
regrettably
mistaken a beginning
for an ending.

Feeling its maniacal smile
engulfing my racing heart,
igniting sparks in my chest,
tapping chills down my spine,
I strain as
it warns,
provokes,
demands:

Didn't you know?

We
    are
        just
            getting
                started.

    The *true* unsettling
has yet to come.

Unsettling
Recently,
each night
after I've done an
exhausting number of rituals
that blur the boundaries between
self-care and compulsion,
and close my eyes,
counting my breaths,
mindfully bringing
present-moment awareness
to the sensations of air
caressing my lips,
slipping down,
deep into my core,
and spilling out again,
just when I find my mind
starting to calm
and the ticker-tape of running,
racing thoughts,
intrusive images,
and visceral pangs
of dread, paranoia,
and anxiety
beginning to settle
ever so slightly,
there is this fleeting moment
of silence, of stillness,
of ease.
In the time it takes for me

to become conscious of this peace,
a haunting, terrifying fear
comes over me as I notice
voices getting louder
and louder
inside
my mind.
They start as only a few,
all in a whisper,
practically indecipherable,
voices that are
quiet in volume
but chillingly
loud in their validity,
their manipulative
resemblance to reality,
calling me further
into the landscape
of the disturbing uncertainty,
the tormenting unreliability
of the here
and now.
At first,
hearing these voices
shook me to my core
because they
seeped out of the remote
corners of my mind,
gaps between convictions
and crevices

between consciousness
that I could never
access during the day,
could never see before,
could never prove existed
since my mind,
my bodymind
is continuously erupting with
clashing thoughts,
conflicting feelings,
consuming sensations,
all of which
bear *my* voice,
my tone,
my inflection,
my hopes,
my dreams,
my trepidations,
that are decisively,
unquestionably
me.
These new nightly voices,
that only began
coming out
of the shadows,
through the shadows,
within the shadows -
unwanted byproducts
of years and years of practice
cultivating

briefly,
desperately,
transiently
a still, quiet mind -
did not sound like me,
look like me,
feel like me.
They were other peoples' voices,
all different, each unique,
night after night,
coming in droves,
talking over one another,
never to one another,
building in intensity,
in volume,
in need
to be heard,
disembodied,
without form or substance,
shouting into the void of a mind
with an audience of one
who desperately desired
solitude
in the moments
before sleep;
moments that have
always overwhelmed
me with irrational dread
and panic, not knowing
what would happen,

how it would happen,
or if I would survive this happening
without falling, plunging
into another world,
some elsewhere
of obscurity
with no path,
no guide,
and no promise
of returning to consciousness,
forced to live within
a panic so big,
so vast,
that I am certain
that even if a part of me
gives in,
accepts this fear,
this space,
this place,
this possibility
to be true,
I will never, ever
be able to withstand
crossing
the unknown
terrain that exists
between the worlds of
wakefulness and dreams.
Despite having traversed
this portal

successfully
night after night
since I was born,
the doubt, the fear,
the terror
still remains.
My therapist encouraged me
to bring curiosity to these voices,
invite them to share,
to speak,
to be seen,
to be heard
by me.
So, with interest and apprehension,
as I turn off my light,
kiss my partner good night,
put in my earplugs,
and place a covering over my eyes,
(crucial elements to my sleep practice
if I am to avoid
enduring middle of the night
panic attacks,
staying awake all night
listening for intruders,
or agonizing over my perpetual fears
of being bombed
that occur each time
a plane flies overhead,
waking and checking
over and over again for postings

about the attack
that we must be under, furious as to why
it has not been picked up by the local news
yet—*what are they waiting for?!*),
I settle into my body and all that it has to hold
finding myself, now,
oddly eager for these voices,
unknowable as they may be,
seeking their companionship
in the moments before slumber
that I find most terrifying, lonely,
and uncertain.
Ironically, by shutting out
all external sound,
I can hear them better,
a bit more clearly,
a bit more soundly,
and, although they do not feel
part of me and exist beyond
the realm of my control,
there is something comforting
about their consistency,
their constancy,
and the fact that they
choose me,
visit me,
never demand anything more of me
than to *be*,
to breathe,
and to listen,

filling my awareness like
the undulating cacophony
of a crowded café,
always intriguing,
occasionally unsettling
depending on what
I overhear,
realizing that my mind
never ceases to construct
lives and worlds
all of its own,
inviting me to be both passenger
and vessel for its
mystery and
awe,
tricking me into thinking,
time and again,
that I have the power to truly
know it
when my mind,
like a haunting,
is always one step ahead
of all knowing,
of all becoming.
The more I befriend these voices,
the more capable I am of finding
humor in their fragmented
soliloquies,
one of which,
just the other night,

in the mere
fractions of a second before
I drifted away into sleep,
screamed at the top
of its lungs my birth name,
a deadname that I despise,
that burns my skin when
directed my way,
that I got rid of,
for good,
(or so I thought)
a few years ago. Gasping
awake, rattled by the recognition
of experiencing this harm that
hadn't occurred for quite some time,
I, surprisingly, found a sly smile
unfurl across my face,
ready to take flight,
and a light chuckle
spew out of my mouth.
Settling back down,
easing my body back into
a semblance of calm,
I shook my head from side to side,
still smirking,
and finally, after months of silent,
patient,
compassionate listening,
I replied, *You bastard!*
and fell back to sleep,

the voices momentarily dulled
and shocked at the rise
they had finally gotten out
of me. I wonder, through
confrontation,
through friction,
what secrets,
knowings,
understandings,
may yet to be released
the deeper and deeper
I go into the moments,
the interstices,
between wakefulness
and sleep,
between being
and becoming:

> To follow Aguilar's turn toward the boulder [in her photograph, *Grounded #114* (2006)]...is not to turn away from questions of objectification or dehumanization; it is rather, to consider how these questions already anticipate the contemporary "nonhuman turn"—to examine...not how the "boundaries between human and nonhuman melt away" but how those categories rub on, and against, each other, generating *friction* and *leakage* [emphasis added]. And it is also to ask about other forms, other worlds, other ways of being that might emerge from the transmaterial affections suggested in the photograph. When the "sub-human, in-human, non-human" queer actively connects with the

other-than-human, what might that connection spawn?
(Luciano & Chen, 2015, p. 186)

What might that connection
call forth,
bring forth,
unearth
for us all
if only
we are receptive
enough to receive
it?

Receive
As a peer support volunteer,
I was asked by someone,
a complete stranger
not much older than myself,
if it was possible to be trans
and to not have known from birth.
This oftentimes singular narrative
of trans becoming that this person
referenced as having been used to invalidate
their recent coming to know[2] experience (Davis, 2021)
wreaks havoc
on and within a vast community whose
identities and relationships to
gender *norms,*

dysphoria,
euphoria,
and *trauma*
defy definitive scripts,
narratives that have so often been written,
ghost written,
by cisgender clinicians
whose diagnostic "criteria
permit a semblance of knowability
(trans people innately feel *this* way),
while the contradictory traumatizing
reality can be maintained unscathed
(gender is uncertain, its affects and
genealogies are unclear)" (Wiggins, 2020, p. 69).
These diagnoses perpetuate
the ideologies of
a medical model of disability
that demands a "problem" to be known,
biologically based,
decontextualized from interconnected
systemic injustices
and these systems' internalizations
and socializations
within, between, and through
each and every one of us,
all in order for this *"problem,"*
this bodymind,
to be identified,
categorized, and,
ultimately,

"cured" through the imposed
 framework of a white
 supremacist,
 settler colonial binary
 gendered ontology
 and sanist forms
 of knowledge production.
 Asking about my own experiences
 coming out and navigating
 socially and medically transitioning
 as an adult, this person wondered
 if I had known that I was trans
 as a young child. Closing my eyes
 and taking a deep,   long   breath,
 I began to chart the expansive
 realm of my trans
 (un)knowability,
 something that I had been struggling
 to do since realizing my own
 trans identity not too long ago.
 (A realization that solidified for me under the I-93 overpass,
 sitting in the driver's seat of my car
 in my school's staff parking lot
 after a long,
 excruciating day of being called Ms. *over* and *over*
 and *over* again. With cars whizzing above me
 and the saltwater breeze of the bay
 intermingling with the hot,
 suffocating smog of the city's traffic
 spilling in through my car windows,

I was immobile, "stuck" as I often call episodes like these,
incapable of moving a muscle,
while time passed around me,
the fear and uncertainty of what my life would become
washing over me,
sucking me under,
swallowing me whole.)
Each memory that rose to the surface
of my consciousness
and bodily awareness
was indeed a moment of trans knowing,
of gender nonconforming revelation,
of definitive nonbinary exploration,
"[h]aunting[ly] rais[ing] specters"
while "alter[ing] the experience of being
in time, the way we separate the past,
the present, and the future" (Gordon, 2008, p. xvi).
Despite not bearing a trans label,
it was abundantly clear to me
that my young bodymind
defined these moments,
(some so fleeting they occupied no more
yet so, *so* much more
than a flash,
a gasp,
a flicker
of cognition),
in ways that defied the
boundaries of linguistic classification.
Redefining my early *visceral*

binary gender-disruptive experiences
through the boundless framework of
possibilities for identity and expression,
I found that, although my young self
did not possess the language
to help make this knowability
explicitly known
to a gender nonconforming community
who could
and *would*
eventually embrace me as one
of their own,
it was in this time
when I lacked access to *specific*
trans-specific knowledge
that those within the
medical industrial complex remained fortified
as gatekeepers to trans pathways
to trans affirming care that, for me,
was everything I needed for
trans becoming,
trans belonging,
and *trans* survival.
When I began to answer this person,
this *no longer* a stranger's
question, I invited us both to settle
into this space, this place
of complexity,
of liminality,
and seeming contradiction

where I explained that I *did not*
and absolutely *did*
(with every fiber of my being)
know
that I was trans when I was a child.
Although it took me 31 years
to say these words out loud,
(*I am transgender*)
their meaning had been etched deep,
deep within my veins since
my consciousness first
collided into a body
that would become a vessel
to a socialized destination to which I
was never intended to go.
I described recalling these distinct
moments of knowing
that do not fit normative
scripts but were, nonetheless,
real,
valid,
loud,
and *so, so* clear...

How long did it take me to develop the
skills and tools to trust and listen?

Too long *and,*
just long enough.

•

I remember a scene from a home video
from a birthday long,
long ago
where I was opening a box
and inside was a dress
with bright colors and frills.
As soon as I caught sight of the
box's contents,
I instantly broke down
crying, screaming,
yelling, looking up at the camera,
hysterically,
imploringly,
longingly
to be seen,
and heard.
My parents, watching the video alongside me,
remarked at how
ungrateful I was and how terrible
this outburst had made
my hard-working grandparents feel
about the present they had so generously
gotten me. It took me years to
connect those cries and visible
expressions of pain that I saw
written across my face,
pouring out of my eyes,
to the days

in high school
of desperately trying to push the boundaries
of a highly gendered dress code,
forced to wear women's clothes and feel
my skin burn, my brain go foggy,
my knees shake,
dissociating from a self
in search of a self
that I didn't yet know was possible,
that I didn't yet recognize was plausible,
that I didn't yet believe existed,
for I had never seen *it* before,

I had never seen *them* before,

I had never seen *me* before.

•

The best way that I could describe
this knowing to
this person, recognizing that language
was illusive,
insufficient,
incomplete,
was to say that,
just because as children
we did not arrive at the moment
where we are today, defining ourselves
as trans, nonbinary, and gender nonconforming,

does not mean that we are somehow
deficient,
uncertain,
too *late* to the game.
Instead, perhaps our experiences
are indicative
of the expansive nature of trans knowing,
of trans becoming
that has always existed
regardless of terminology
or access to representation.
And what, I wonder,
might occur when we
begin to view our experiences
as not isolated
solely within the world of gender
identity and expression,
but rather,
deeply situated within a complex
matrix of social locations
and identities that are all interconnected
to systems of advantage and inequity
that impact the ways in which we navigate
spaces, places, people, and time,
all in the search of futures
that will ensure our individual
and collective survival.
As a child, no one told me there was a door
to a world
that was made just for me

or people like me,
or people I had always hoped
to become.
And, if I didn't
know that this door existed,
how was I expected to look for it,
let alone find it?
And so, yes, it did take me time,
three decades of time,
to get here,
moments that I sometimes
look back on
with grief and despair,
wishing I had spent more years
arriving as opposed to
becoming.
But,
this is my journey
and to each part of me
and to each member of our community
who act as signposts
guiding me here,
guiding so many
of us here
to a *now*
that was inconceivable
to me *then*,
I extend the utmost
compassion,
gratitude,

and love.
I
owe
them
everything.
And, perhaps,
as we continue to tell our stories,
as unique as they may be,
as *(un)*conventional as they
may be,
may they swirl,
meld,
and fold into the vast sea of trans
narratives that help us believe
and *know*
that the *trans*gressive worlds
we currently inhabit
have always existed
and
will always exist.
May these narratives,
our narratives,
continue to
manifest as bridges,
ramps,
portals,
and pathways
for trans folks
who follow
that connect every

elsewhere to a here,
a there,
an everywhere,
ensuring that
no one
is ever lost
again.
We can't be lost
if we already call ourselves
home...

All knowledge is good knowledge, [the creature] said.
I don't know if that's true...It doesn't feel true right now.
Truth does not care if it feels true or not. It is true nonetheless.
(Emezi, 2019, p. 140)

Nonetheless
A few summers ago,
not long after the first season of *Pose*
came out,
(a show that I couldn't wait to see
but knew that I needed the right time,
the right place,
the right headspace
to fully take in),
I was recovering from top surgery
and looking for everything and anything
to watch to take my mind off of the pain.

This surgery
pushed me forward on the path
to living,
breathing,
and being
the person that I had always thought
I had been,
but whose masculine-perceived expression
would be cruelly denied of me
every time that I looked into a mirror
or caught my reflection
in a storefront window.
These illusory manifestations,
machinations,
of my gender dysphoria
seemed to take
sick pleasure over the past 31 years
in reminding me that
that which I saw
was by no means
that which you saw,
complicated plays on a nonbinary
reality that was
trying to make itself known
and avowed
within a broader internal landscape
of delusion
that was terrifyingly amplified
by my yet understood
but deeply felt and sincerely known

symptoms of OCD, bipolar II,
and PTSD,[3]
diagnoses that were still
far, *far* out of reach.

Looking back now
on the decades that I missed
of living as my true self,
how could I possibly
have rationalized, concretized,
valorized,
a transgender identity
that seeped and swirled
within my bodymind
that was fully suffused
with Madness, a Madness
whose voices continuously
had to be distressingly
excluded
from coming out
narratives if I wanted
my gender identity
to be believed,
trusted, and affirmed? Even though
my gender dysphoria is still
complicatedly and
problematically labeled
as a mental disorder
in the same text that holds
my OCD, bipolar, and PTSD diagnoses,

I knew that my trans and Mad coming out
stories would invalidate each other
and, seeing as there was not another day
that I was willing to live
as someone "yet to be born"
and, thus, "already dead" (Grace, 2014, 1:11),
it was clear, early on, that
to be truly free,
I would have to disavow parts of me
that tried desperately,
helplessly,
hopelessly
to claw their way out
from the suffocating
depths of my reluctant,
heartbreaking
Mad refusal
and suppression:

> Attempting to balance requests for complete removal with concerns surrounding access to care, the new designation "gender dysphoria" garners an entire section in the *DSM*, finally physically apart from the paraphilias…(APA 2013)…In a way that closely mirrors the history of pathologizing homosexuality (Drescher 2010; Ross 2015), nonnormative identity is no longer, in itself, an adequate basis for diagnosis and is therefore not considered inherently perverse or disordered. Rather, an individual's suffering and conflict with their gender has been concretized as the requisite and differentiating characteristic of mental illness. (Wiggins, 2020, p. 61)

Waking up from surgery
and looking down on my chest below,
I felt a peace that was more blissful than
any I could have previously fathomed.
It was as if the apparitions,
the feelings of wholeness
that permeated
the moments before
I was crushed each time
by the sight of my reflection
were now true to form,
true to life.
As the lines between the real and the unreal
blurred right before my eyes,
my debilitating longing
for a trans imaginary
that never felt like anything more
than a fleeting elsewhere
that could never be
for it never was,
was finally making itself tangible,
corpo*real,*
solid,
confirming my gendered existence
via a surgical removal
of body parts that,
unbeknownst to me,
had been the true delusion all along.
Who knew that I would find completeness
within an embodied absence.

It was thus, during this period
of post-surgery recovery
that abruptly
took me away
from the LGBTQ2IA+[4]
mental health facility
where I had been receiving care
that month prior
after a full and complete
mental breakdown,
that I sat in bed
flipping through my Netflix queue,
looking to escape,
for at least a little while,
from the deeply interwoven web
of transness and Madness
that was blossoming inside of me,
growing from roots that had taken hold
many,
many
years ago.
I soon stumbled upon *American Horror Story*,
a show that I had previously refused to watch
because, when you find the world
to be utterly terrifying,
wholly unbearable,
full of countless people, places, and things,
    (*all* nouns, really)
that should be avoided
at all costs,

there's, ultimately,
no need
to dedicate time
to watching horror films
and shows…
I'm already the protagonist
in a story that I am certain will have
a haunting ending to match its
frightening beginning.
Thus, stories of horror and gore,
particularly those that play on the tenuous boundary
between the real and the unreal,
the definitively occurred and the
just because it didn't technically happen
doesn't mean it couldn't absolutely happen
right here
right now
to me,
only create more fodder
for my obsessive,
compulsive,
occasionally hallucinatory,
sometimes psychotic,
and perpetually paranoid mind,
especially when
that which we are meant to fear
is cinematically represented
time and again
by individuals with bodyminds and expressions
that *transgress*

societally constructed notions
of normativity.
How often must I be reminded to fear
aspects of myself that are still in a state
of becoming?
With this in mind, I realized that,
remarkably enough,
both *Pose* and *American Horror Story*
had the same creators;
perhaps this show might be
different. *I want this show to be different.*
Drawn to season 5's title, *Hotel,*
by an eerie fixation on revisiting my obsession
with what Madness
laid behind the doors of
the Overlook, the ominous
hotel setting of Stanley
Kubrick's 1980 film,
The Shining,
(a film that also defined
for my childhood mind
society's conception of Madness
as something to be feared,
criminalized, and pathologized,
especially when combined
with the aggression of a masculine
protagonist who portrayed
to me one of the few representations
of Mad masculinity,
a gendered version of self

that now awaited me daily with
each application
of my testosterone gel[5]),
I apprehensively began watching
the first episode of the season
and, not long after the opening scenes,
we are introduced to
Liz Taylor, a visibly gender nonconforming
character who reveals,
later in the season,
that she is transfeminine,
gracing the Hotel Cortez,
where she resides,
with her flowing beauty.
Given the ease and poise
with which she navigates the hotel,
moving through spaces that had
just previously been filled
with grotesque imagery,
Liz Taylor acts as a breathtaking,
sublime counterpoint
to the monstrosity
and horrors that exist around her.
However, despite this being the reality
of these introductory scenes,
this was by no means how
I originally remember
this character being portrayed.
Perhaps because I was still
heavily sedated during my top surgery recovery,

perhaps because I was still terrified
of my trans *and* nonbinary
gender journey ahead,
perhaps because I struggle
to watch horror films
and not be overwhelmed
with the fear, guilt,
worry, and delusion
that I *must have* done *that* to someone,
I *must* be capable of such atrocious acts,
(and, even if I know that I *absolutely*
did not commit such crimes,
pernicious doubt still persists,
and intrusive thoughts flood
my mind, over and over,
convincing me
that the imaginary
is real
and that the real
has now become an endless
nightmare
with *no doors* to open,
no room to escape),
perhaps...
I distinctly recall Liz Taylor as
horrifyingly being
portrayed as the monster,
the villain,
the brutal, merciless butcher
who claims the lives of the

season's first guests.
Rewatching this episode now
and realizing how profoundly
my memory has deceived me,
yet again,
I am filled with such sincere
terror and dread at my bodymind's
ability to twist truth into fiction.
It is clear to me that
I could not help but associate
Liz Taylor's presence
in the Hotel Cortez
with my childhood experiences
of watching *The Shining*
and all that I embodied
and viscerally remembered
from the film's final moments
when Wendy, the wife of Jack,
the film's protagonist,
witnesses a man, one of the hotel's
ghostly guests and/or
a delusional byproduct of Wendy's mind,
in a tuxedo
receiving oral sex
from someone hidden behind
the guise of a
bear costume.
Wielding a large butcher
knife as she rushes through
the hotel after helping her

son, Danny, escape
from his murderously
maniacal father,
Wendy becomes
dizzy with horror as she
backpedals away from such
"unsettling" imagery,
gasping between rapid breaths
that seem
to elude her.
This scene, which breaks the fourth wall
for a disturbingly long period of time,
and when considered in the context
of Kubrick's film as a whole,
left a tragically powerful
impact on my notion
of what and *who*
should be feared
and how seamlessly
my queerness and gender non-normativity,
let alone my Madness,
would fit into the room that,
with a mere glance at
its occupants' deviant deeds,
filled Wendy with disgust
and repulsion:

> ...hotels are at their very core unhomely places. They are
> places to be at home and yet not home; they are familiar and
> unfamiliar at the same time. Freud describes the uncanny

"as that species of the frightening that goes back to what was
once well known and had long been familiar" (124) but this
familiarity is now brought back into direct view and the un-
canny "applies to everything that was intended to remain
secret, hidden away, and has come into the open." (Gordon,
2019, p. 149)

Knowing that, over the course
of the season,
Liz Taylor
manages to live her truth,
being born into a world
that is full of endless death,
countless horrors
which she comes to denounce,
remaining a beacon of stability
and tenderness,
eventually a transcestor
who is, herself,
in the final moments
of the season,
mercifully relieved
of her physical and emotional suffering,
I cannot help but reflect on how it is
that I, in my initial viewing
of this show,
expected the only trans
character to be portrayed as the monster
when, in actuality,
the true killer, the ultimate villain

in this season,
spares Liz Taylor's
life, choosing
to take the lives of his victims
due to *their* perceived moral
transgressions, deviance,
and deception.
Will I be similarly
spared as well?
Drowning in the depths
of my internalized
transphobia that spilled
to the surface in the midst of
the early days of my own
medical and social transition,
I allowed my deeply
seated fears
to be projected
onto this character,
expecting her to be
depraved,
viewing her in the ways
that I was terrified of society
viewing
me.
Thus, I am left wondering
how my viewing of
Mad and trans
and gender nonconforming
representation

on screen swirls
and melds with the
Mad trans world
"that's raging inside
of me" (Grace, 2014, 2:30),
bearing the traces
and hauntings
of my Madness
and gender identity
origin stories,
and, also,
absorbing and buoying
my ever-evolving
Mad and trans self
in the thoroughly
situated context
of my privileges
and oppressions,
"stereotypes and shame" (Clare, 2017, p. 177).
How do the representations that I see
reflect back that which
I *want* to see,
dread to see,
have seen
and have *yet* to see
and acknowledge as *true*
and emblematic of my own
embodied knowing?
When I reflect on how
trans and Mad representation

has changed,
I must also unpack the ways
that I have changed in relation
to it, in relation to those around me,
and society at large,
and how my internalizations
of socializations,
of desires,
of aversions,
are never truly solely internal
and interweave with that which
I continue to perceive on screens,
in mirrors,
in the reflections of storefront windows,
redefining the ways in which
I attempt to explore
the ever-evolving nature
of self
as possibility,
as limitation.
How does my own longing to see
behind the doors of
the Overlook Hotel
and the Hotel Cortez
equate to my longing to uncover
hidden truths within my own self
and finally open that which
has remained shut for far
too long?

Interstices: A Poetic Afterword
What happens in the gaps,
cracks,
holes,
and hinges,
between the familiar
and the hidden,
the seen and the
unseen, the homely
and the not yet home (Gordon, 2019, p. 149)?
It is in the "interstices
of discursive practices
and at the collapse of generic
categories" (Stryker, 1994, p. 248)
that I find comfort and seek
to reside, for
despite the messy
interlacing
of my Mad and
trans subjectivities
which are perpetually,
precariously
situated within
"a field governed by
the unstable but indissoluble
relationship between language
and materiality" (Stryker, 1994, p. 248),
I still find myself
"constantly polic[ing]
the boundary constructed

by [my] own founding
in order to maintain the functions of
'inside' and 'outside' against a regime
of signification/materialization
whose intrinsic instability produces
the rupture of subjective boundaries" (Stryker, 1994, p. 248),
boundaries that, for me, are
often impossible to map,
since where one
realized part of me begins,
another desperately
seeks
to end.
When constantly
questioning the borders
between the real and the unreal,
the valid and the invalid,
the apparent and the obscure,
forcing myself
to define myself
in the midst of this ambiguity,
ease can slip so effortlessly
into *dis*-ease,
and what
seems possible,
definitively graspable,
ultimately achievable,
highly believable,
can so discouragingly,
effortlessly,

suddenly,
dissolve back into the
ether of delusion,
denial,
and disgrace.
Despite confronting
these terrifying
complexities
on the choppy
road to
and through
my Mad and trans becoming,
I recognize that,
if it were not for the gaps,
cracks,
holes,
and hinges
that constitute the
interstices of my being,
which is endlessly
shifting, forming,
eroding, and
combusting,
there would be no space,
no place,
for light to
seep in,
creep in,
"generating friction
and leakage" (Luciano & Chen, 2015, p. 186)

with the shadows,
in the shadows,
between the shadows,
forging
the fragments,
traces,
and ghosts,
of selves
that have
been waiting
to be revealed
well before I
ever knew
that the true purpose
of my fractures
and fissures
were to hold,
embrace,
invite,
and welcome
all that is still to come
in my
boundless
journey
to wholeness
and completion.

NOTES

1   I find it critical to address the ocularcentrism of my use of the word "see" as representative of knowing, witnessing, believing, and understanding. As someone with able-bodied privilege, I seek to actively disrupt ableism on a systemic, interpersonal, and internalized level. By drawing on the Emezi (2019) quotation that follows which comes from their extraordinarily powerful young adult novel, *Pet*, I hope to allude to Emezi's construction of a creature named Pet who, without the possession of eyes, connects and communicates with the world around them from a deeply embodied, visceral, relational, ancestral, and ethereal realm. Thus, my use of the word "see" throughout this piece is intended to defy ocularcentric boundaries and meld into worlds of knowing that never have to be visible to be perceived.

2   I want to extend my utmost gratitude and appreciation to my colleague and Syracuse University Intergroup Dialogue co-facilitator, Easton Davis, whose critical dialogic pedagogy and scholarship on coming to know processes, embodied forms of knowledge production, and the transgressive, liberatory praxis of marginalized bodyminds within extractive, neoliberal, predominantly and historically white educational institutions, has left and continues to leave invaluable imprints on my own autoethnographic methodology and scholarly journey. To explore more of his work on coming to know, I highly recommend reading Davis's (2021) forthcoming article, "Reclaiming the Body: Racial Embodiment and Emotions as a Pedagogical Practice in Intergroup Dialogue."

3   Although I am sharing my diagnoses here, I also want to acknowledge the privilege and profound complexity of diagnosis

and access to diagnosis, a theme that I attempt to grapple with throughout this piece and in previous scholarship, including "Hauntings of Longing: A Mad Autoethnographic Poetic Transcription" (Cosantino, in press). This grappling which, for me, has no end and no resolution, perpetually requires intense criticality and reflection on my own situatedness, especially as an able-bodied white person with class and citizenship privilege, within the vast national and transnational context of the medical industrial complex and its current and historical relationship to violence, cure, anti-Blackness, anti-Indigeneity, carcerality, coloniality, disablism, and erasure. As Jasbir Puar (2017) describes in *The Right to Maim: Debility, Capacity, and Disability*, it is crucial to recognize that the "access to the identity of disability...is a function, result, and reclamation of white privilege" (p. 15) and that "debility [is] endemic, perhaps even normative, to disenfranchised communities: not normative, not exceptional, not that which is to come or can be avoided, but a banal feature of quotidian existence that is already definitive of the precarity of that existence" (p. 16). Although I view my diagnoses with contention, my access to these diagnoses is still connected to a global, imperial, neoliberal medical industrial complex that enacts precarity and debility that I must assume responsibility for perpetuating. Furthermore, in my attempts to contribute to Mad scholarship, this criticality remains essential to actively disrupting and dismantling the white supremacy that permeates the Mad movement. As Mad and queer scholars and activists of color, such as Rachel Gorman, annu saini, Louise Tam, Onyinyechukwu Udegbe, and Onar Usar (2013) powerfully describe in their "Mad People Of Colour: A Manifesto," which was shared with me by my remarkable colleague

Kristian Contreras, doctoral candidate in Cultural Foundations of Education at Syracuse University, the continued centering of whiteness within the Mad movement acts as an extension of the same systemic violence, silencing, and erasure that the Mad movement seeks to challenge. Thus, my grappling with diagnoses that were given to me through a white, Western, colonial psy-framework and my access to such diagnoses are not neutral and are inextricably linked to larger systems of harm, privilege, and exclusion.

4 LGBTQ2IA+ stands for Lesbian, Gay, Bisexual, Transgender, Queer/Questioning, Two Spirit, Intersex, Asexual, and the ever-evolving language for nonbinary identities and expressions.

5 I expand on these themes and their relationship to a Mad and trans methodology in much more detail in my piece entitled, "Epiphanic Haunting: An Autoethnographic Origin Story of Madness and Gender Nonconformity," submitted for publication.

REFERENCES

Clare, E. (2017). Brilliant imperfection: Grappling with cure. Duke University Press. http://dx.doi.org/10.1215/9780822373520-212

Cosantino, J. (in press). Hauntings of longing: A Mad autoethnographic poetic transcription. *Disability Studies Quarterly.*

Davis, E. J. (2021). *Reclaiming the body: Racial embodiment and emotions as a pedagogical practice in intergroup dialogue.* Manuscript submitted for publication.

Emezi, A. (2019). *Pet.* Make Me a World.

Gordon, A. F. (2008). Ghostly matters: Haunting and the sociological imagination. Minneapolis: University of Minnesota Press.

Gordon, R. (2019). America's deadliest hotel: The gender politics of checking in and never leaving. In Earle, H. E. H., *Gender, sexuality and queerness in american horror story: Critical essays*. McFarland & Company, Inc.

Gorman, R., saini, a., Tam, L., Udegbe, O., & Usar, O. (2013). Mad People Of Colour: A Manifesto. *Asylum: The Magazine for Democratic Psychiatry, 20*(4), 27.

Grace, L. J. (2014). FUCKMYLIFE666. On *Transgender dysphoria blues*. Total Treble and Xtra Mile Recordings.

Grace, L. J. (2014). True trans soul rebel. On *Transgender dysphoria blues*. Total Treble and Xtra Mile Recordings.

Luciano, D., & Chen, M. Y. (2019). Queer inhumanisms. *GLQ: A Journal of Lesbian and Gay Studies, 25*(1), 113-117. doi: 10.1215/10642684-7275600

Minh-Ha, T. T. (2009). Woman, native, other: Writing postcoloniality and feminism. Indiana University Press.

Puar, J. K. (2017). *The right to maim: Debility, capacity, disability*. Durham: Duke University Press.

Stryker, S. (1994). My words to Victor Frankenstein above the village of Chamounix: Performing transgender rage. *GLQ: A Journal of Lesbian and Gay Studies, 1*(3), 237–254. https://doi.org/10.1215/10642684-1-3-237

Wiggins, T. B. D. (2021). A perverse solution to misplaced distress: Trans subjects and clinical disavowal. *Transgender Studies Quarterly, 7*(1), 56-76. https://doi.org/10.1215/23289252-7914514

coming out twice: how my "nuclear meltdown" helped me embrace my madness and autism

DR. BENJAMIN HABIB

My entire body was heating up. My muscles were heavy, and my skin began to vibrate as if being shocked by a mild electric current. With every question they asked I struggled even more as my mind and body began to shut down. Finally, I gave in and said, "I can't do this." The interviewers quickly cut to the next story. I sat there immobilised, in complete shock. What the hell just happened?

I'm an expert on North Korea's nuclear weapons program, but in 2016 I had my own "nuclear meltdown" while being interviewed about North Korea on live television. This chapter is a reflection on my televised Chernobyl moment and how this ended up being a moment of transmutation, a catalysing event that led me to "come out" twice, as Mad, and then as autistic.

THE INTERVIEW ON LIVE TV

I'm an academic in the field of International Relations, with a research specialty on North Korea. My PhD thesis examined North Korea's nuclear weapons program, an area not even remotely linked to mental health. I've delivered hundreds of lectures and public presentations and talked about my research on radio. I'd even done prior TV interviews, including one with the same *ABC News 24* network in 2015, where I talked down the barrel of a camera in a small, darkened room for a live cross to a studio in Sydney.

When I was contacted by a producer from the ABC Melbourne studio on a Sunday afternoon in 2016 with an invitation to appear on the show *ABC News Breakfast* the following morning, I gladly accepted. It's not the first time I'd appeared on TV and I was confident in offering comment on my area of expertise. After all, isn't sharing our research with the public what academics are supposed to do? Plus, *ABC News Breakfast* was a program I watched each morning, and I was excited about the prospect of appearing on the show.

I should have fucking known better. Every time I've ever said yes to a public engagement, I've immediately felt a hole open up in the pit of my stomach, and this occasion was no exception. My physical discomfort steadily grew from that initial reaction at the moment I said "yes" to the interview, to the moment on set when *ABC News Breakfast* co-host Michael Rowland threw me his first question in the interview.

It was a long fifteen hours between invitation and interview. I watched an NBA basketball game on TV that Sunday night, but I couldn't tell you who played or recall a single detail about the game. I was so wired. As Sunday PM ticked over to Monday AM, I was ruminating over what I would say in the interview, what I would wear and how I would get to the ABC studio for the 7:00

AM interview time slot. When I boarded a train to commute to the Melbourne CBD early that Monday morning, I hadn't slept at all.

I arrived at the ABC's Melbourne studio in Southbank forty minutes before the scheduled interview time. As usual, I'd given myself ample time for the commute to buffer against potential misfortune. I get super-anxious when I have to travel somewhere new, especially whenever mass transit is involved. I find all the people, the waiting, and the security and surveillance innately stressful. Even for someone as well-travelled as myself, I always find transit hubs like train stations and airports stressful environments for me to be in.

I checked in at the security desk and waited about ten minutes before a member of the *News Breakfast* production team escorted me upstairs. I was taken into a dressing room to have my "TV face" applied, getting daubed with make-up. The make-up artist was amazingly friendly, but in hindsight my inability to say anything cogent in small talk was another red flag that something wasn't right.

From the dressing room I was taken into an expansive open-plan office, where the presenters and support crew do all their off-set work. There I waited for about twenty-five minutes, absent-mindedly scanning old newspapers and watching the hum of activity in the office. I picked at the cuticles on my fingers, as I often do, while repeating in my mind what I wanted to say about North Korea in the interview. I was concentrating on breathing deeply and sitting still, but became even more agitated with the effort. Fuck, why did I arrive so early!

About two minutes before my interview, I was guided into the studio's production control room, which looked like a miniaturised NASA mission control, packed with TV screens, computer monitors, and other equipment crammed into an otherwise small, dark room. It was a buzzing hive of fast-paced, urgent activity.

As the story prior to my interview was airing, I was led into the studio itself where I was mic'ed up and seated next to co-hosts Virginia Trioli and Michael Rowland. They both quickly introduced themselves and shook my hand.

I'd watched this show every morning for ten years and was familiar with the desk that I was now sitting at. What I wasn't prepared for was all the technology that doesn't appear on-screen. There were television monitors and computer screens embedded in the desk, hidden from camera view. There were numerous other TV's, auto-prompters and cameras all around me in the studio, pointing directly at me. I felt immediately claustrophobic under the oppressive sensory overload in this space.

The lead-in story to my interview was a piece on the American reaction to a North Korean rocket launch. There was a clip of U.S. White House spokesperson Sam Powers delivering an official statement. I remember thinking that I'd cite Powers' remarks in my comments. I knew what I was going to say. "I've got this," I kept telling myself, while also longing to get the interview over with so I could go home and get some sleep.

As the Sam Powers clip ended and the tech crew counted in the live camera feed to the studio desk, I could feel my body over-load with adrenaline. My entire body was heating up. My muscles got heavy and my skin began to vibrate as if being shocked with a mild electric current.

Michael Rowland introduced me and then turned in my direction to ask his first question. I knew I had the answer to his question, but it was like the file with my response had been deleted from my brain. My mind was suddenly swimming in a haze.

As I realised that seconds were ticking away without me forming a coherent answer, the physical reactions intensified. I babbled and stumbled, my carefully prepared comments slipping away from conscious awareness. Michael and Virginia, seeing that I was struggling, asked prompting questions in an effort help me out of the hole. Yet with every question they asked I struggled even more as my body and mind shut down.

Finally, I gave in and said, "I can't do this," and Michael and the editors quickly threw to the next story. I sat there immobilised, in complete shock.

Virginia grabbed my arm after the live feed cut away and said, "don't worry, it's OK." And that was it. I was led out of the studio room by one of the production team, who was also kind and supportive, as were the staff in the editing room. But they had a job to get on with, and I was left alone to grapple with what had just occurred.

I struggle even now to describe that feeling of shock in moments immediately after the interview. I was numb, I didn't have the words, because there were none. Someone from the production team led me back out into the lobby and offered me a coffee in the cafeteria, but I felt so terrible that I fled the building directly.

All I wanted to do was crawl into a hole, away from people, away from judgement. Instead, I boarded a train packed with morning peak hour commuters for the forty-minute journey back home. For the remainder of the day I was shaken, upset, and terrified of the ridicule that awaited me on social media. Eventually my anxiety symptoms subsided enough that I managed an hour or two of disturbed sleep.

COMING OUT AS MAD

It was on that train ride home from the ABC studio that morning, with tears welling up in my eyes underneath the protective armour of my sunglasses, that I decided to write about this experience. I would document what I was feeling, a play-by-play account of what my shutdown felt like physically and emotionally as it was happening. It was the only path forward I could see which held the prospect of recovering some dignity.

My biggest fear the following morning was walking down the office corridor at work. The relief I felt at seeing an empty corridor was immense, only to be followed by another wave of anxiety as I turned my office computer to check my email and Twitter feed.

We all know that social media is cesspit, an engine for peoples' righteous indignation and a circus for the memefication of gaffes and misfortunes. There were a couple of trolling tweets on my Twitter feed, though to be honest I found the clumsy stupidity of those tweets more amusing than hurtful, which gave me something to laugh about as I faced the world again. The *Daily Mail* had also done what the *Daily Mail* does and posted video of the interview on their YouTube page as salacious click-bait.

A couple of days after the interview, I published the blog under the title "What it feels like to freeze on national television,"[1] and shared the article on Twitter, as I do with all my blog postings. The tweet quickly went viral because I tagged *ABC News Breakfast* in the tweet. My blog was re-published by several news websites and in the following days I received hundreds of supportive messages from people around the world.

After the positive response to my initial blog, I wrote a series of articles over the course of 2016 on my experiences with anxiety and depression. Some of those writings seem a bit quaint

---

1   Habib. B. "What it feels like to freeze on national television." *Ben@Earth*. 10 February 2016.

now, but they were important to my process of integration from the TV incident.

Making sense of the experience became a scholarly endeavour too. Through my La Trobe University colleague Tessa Zirnsak I discovered Mad Studies, opening me to an academic field which confirmed my intuition that mental health cannot be individual-ised as a personal pathology. Tessa and I co-authored an autoeth-nographic dialogue on madness in the academy,[2] through which I discovered Madness as politics and social movement, as well as lived experience.

Through various healing modalities and introspective work, I came to realise that there was something else underlying my Mad-ness. Yes, I had a long resume of bullying and abuse as a youth, and a history of trauma through my family lineage, but that wasn't enough to explain my lived reality.

Since the mid-2000's I've been relentless in searching for this missing link, this hidden variable that I've always suspected was there but was just outside of view. I've been through Cognitive Be-havioural Therapy, Acceptance and Commitment Therapy, trauma counselling, family of origin therapy, anti-depressant medication, Myers-Briggs personality type indicator, physical modalities in-cluding regular acupuncture, yoga and meditation, shamanic jour-neying and entheogenic plant medicines, journaling, and drawing. All these therapies had benefits, but none of them ultimately an-swered the gnawing existential question of why I felt so different to those around me.

---

2   Zirnsak, T & Habib, B (2022). "Learning from Each Other: An Autoethno-graphic Dialogue on Being Mad in the Academy" in (ed.) C. McGunnigle. *Disability and the Academic Job Market*, Vernon Press, Delaware.

COMING OUT (AGAIN) AS AUTISTIC

I'd been looking in the wrong place. In combing my life history for the wreckage of things done to me, finding plenty of wreckage mind you, I'd missed the ultimate understanding that lay within, in who I am.

It was in a workplace neurodiversity workshop facilitated by another wonderful colleague, autism researcher Elizabeth Radulski, that I first encountered the possibility that I might be autistic. As I pawed away furiously at one of the stimming toys Elizabeth had passed around, I found my physical and emotional experience of the meeting completely transformed. Instead of getting agitated focusing on how loudly I was breathing, or how much saliva was in my mouth, or probing the gaps between my teeth with my tongue, of trying not to play with my pen, or move my legs, or pick at my fingers, I settled into being completely present in the moment. Conscious stimming allowed me to just be. It freed my attention from an exhausting obsession with controlling my body, to being able to take in more of what was going on around me. Mind blown!

The path from light bulb to diagnosis that started in that neurodiversity workshop was paved with self-doubt. As a trial balloon, I tentatively discussed the possibility that I might be autistic with some older relatives, but that did not help to ease my doubt. They were well-meaning, but the sum of their advice was to warn me "not to self-diagnose."

Even though the evidence of my autistic traits was piling up, corroborating my long-held intuition that there was something going on in my psyche, the self-doubt was paralysing: "What if I'm wrong? What if I make a fool of myself?"

This time round, however, I had a grounding in Mad Studies and knew well enough that I'm the expert on myself and that this bread crumb was worth following. I wasn't going to wait for another embarrassing "nuclear meltdown" moment in public to force me in the direction of self-discovery.

The next bread crumb was an article I happened across on Twitter, entitled *"Demolition Girl: On empathy, and being diagnosed with ASD"* by Kara Schlegl.[3] I'd started following Kara's writing after she posted a supportive tweet in response to "What it feels like to freeze on national television." Her journey to autism diagnosis resonated with what I was going through, in a very physical way. My chest began buzzing and warming up, a clear physical reaction to how energised I felt seeing myself reflected in the experience of another person, in reading something that read like it was written specifically for me in that very moment!

I now had enough data points to back up my intuition that it was worth seeking an official diagnosis. However, I'd also heard horror stories of people not being taken seriously and of being screwed around in the mental health system, something I wanted to avoid. I hate bureaucracy so much, not out of any libertarian politics, but because of the significant physical and emotional toll exacted on me every time I interact with one. It's the waiting that gets to me. As I wait in line my anxiety grows, the tell-tale physical sensations of imminent meltdown surge through my body as I rehearse what to say when my number is eventually called.

My first port of call was the organisation AMAZE, the main autistic advocacy group in Victoria. I emailed with some basic ques-

---

3   Schlegl, K. "Demolition Girl: On empathy, and being diagnosed with ASD." *Extremely Brave.* 24 June 2020. https://karaschlegl.substack.com/p/demolition-girl

tions about the process of getting a diagnosis. It might have been easier to call their helpline, but I hate phoning people I don't know; so much stress in figuring out what to say, even for the simplest of inquiries. The response was hearteningly quick but dishearteningly unenlightening: most of the diagnostic services available are for paediatric autism, and that I would have to find a therapist myself with the appropriate expertise for adult diagnosis. They provided a searchable listing of every psychologist and psychiatrist in Victoria, which I briefly browsed but gave up on quickly. We were in Melbourne's first COVID lockdown at this time, which gave me an excuse not to follow up. The lockdown gave me an out to avoid the discomfort of cold calling for help.

A few weeks passed. Melbourne re-opened briefly then transitioned into its second COVID lockdown, which lasted for four months and included significant restrictions on personal movement. In contracting the horizon of my life to the front door, the second COVID lockdown also compelled me to grapple with my paralysing fears and my hopes for liberation from them. Without any other distractions during the lockdown, there was nowhere to withdraw to, nowhere to hide. I had to face this.

My next move was to contact my GP and ask for a referral, reasoning that a GP is likely better able to navigate the health system than I am, and that they'd be able to plug me into the right therapist. The GP was great, he listened empathically to my story and outlined his recommended course of action, providing me with a referral to a local mental health clinic. I was very clear about wanting a psychiatrist with specific expertise in adult autism and he assured me that I'd get what I needed.

Another month passed before my scheduled appointment at the clinic. Because we were on lockdown, the appointment was conducted via a telehealth online platform. Having undergone a lot of previous counselling, I knew that a telehealth consultation was going to be challenging. Instead of the new online video platforms we've become used to in the COVID era like Zoom, the clinic used a video conferencing app that seemed like it was imported from 2002. The audio quality was so bad that we had to speak over the phone to converse properly, as if the video footage was just garnish for a phone conversation. Right from the start, I was immediately uncomfortable with how the consult was progressing. The setting felt unsafe, only amplifying my growing unease through the consultation that the psych on the screen wasn't "hearing me."

The therapist asked me why I was seeking a diagnosis. I responded: "I've endured anxiety and depression for most of my life, but I want to understand why. I've done cognitive behavioural therapy, I've done the trauma work, I've done the family-of-origin work, but there's something else there."

I told him about my profound experience in the neurodiversity workshop earlier in the year, along with the other data points that ultimately compelled me to book this appointment.

Without preamble or explanation, he then launched into the diagnostic questions from the DSM. Luckily, I'd already explored these questions online and knew what he was doing. I was also aware of the many limitations of the DSM diagnostic, and this dude was not making it any easier.

"How was your childhood?" he asked. There's years' worth of counselling embedded in adequately answering that question, what kind of stupid fucking question is that! With every subsequent question I became more agitated. I didn't feel like he was taking me seriously and I got the impression that unless I presented as "Rain Man" he wasn't going to be convinced. As he concluded the questions I was on the verge of tears.

His finding: "You're clearly on the spectrum but you've had a good life, had professional success, it's not a problem. I do think you have anxiety, and I would like to prescribe you some anti-depressant medication."

Motherfucker please. I had begun the consultation telling him that I had anxiety, and his grand conclusion was that I had anxiety and his proposed solution was to drug me up.

"Absolutely not!" I replied. I was furious at his unwillingness to listen, at how he talked down to me like I was a child.

"I'm not a specialist in this area," he said. Wow. Now I felt like I was talking to a child, trying to explain something complex to someone who was clearly not capable of comprehending it.

"This was a colossal waste of time," I responded in exasperation, "I specifically asked my GP for a referral to a psychiatrist with expertise in adult autism, how did I end up with you?" I felt let down by this man. I felt betrayed by my GP, who didn't come through with the referral he promised. But above all else, I was angry at being drawn back into a spiral of crippling self-doubt.

That consultation was an extraordinarily deflating, but is, I'm told, an extremely common experience for adults seeking diagnosis.

But in the bigger picture it wasn't a waste of time at all. I got the confirmation I was looking for, that I was indeed neurodivergent. Autism was the missing link that I always knew was there, just out of reach, but could never quite put my finger on. I'm still processing the enormity of it all, of looking back across my life with a new understanding of how and why I experienced things in the way I did. This chapter is an element of this process of integration.

PART II—INTEGRATION

Just before Melbourne's first COVID lockdown in April 2020 I was invited to speak on a community radio show called "Brainwaves" to talk about my TV meltdown and my life with anxiety. That interview was ultimately postponed because of the lockdown. I often get asked about the TV incident, but that was just one moment in the long arc of my life. So much had changed in my life since that moment, including my interpretation of the event itself.

By the time we rescheduled the interview I had been through the autism diagnosis and had integrated that understanding sufficiently to speak about it publicly. Unlike when I came out as Mad after the TV incident, this disclosure was my conscious choice, a choice that I was confident would be positive for me and be supportive of other neurodivergent people in my orbit.

Reinterpreting the TV incident from the perspectives of Madness and autism has led me to two important insights: (1) the pernicious impact of masking on my sense of self-worth, and (2) the importance of surrounding environmental conditions to my emotional regulation and capacity to interact with others.

GROWING UP "DIFFERENT"

Let's begin with the pernicious impact of masking. When I began my counselling journey in my mid-20's, I realised that my psychological baseline is an exhausting level of heightened situational awareness, not quite fight-or-flight but not far off. I'm intensely tuned in to everything going on around me, while at the same time turning inward to process the flood of high-resolution sensory information from my surrounds. It's like I'm watching Blu-Ray while everyone else is tuned into grainy black-and-white TV. For some time, I thought this was hyper-vigilance related to PTSD. While PTSD is part of the mix, it wasn't enough to explain my sensory overload.

As a kid I found it challenging to figure out how to interact with the world. I felt awkward, looked awkward, and regularly became a target for bullies. Those motherfuckers are like truffle pigs sniffing out difference like it was a mycelial delicacy.

The bullying started in primary school with peers teasing my appearance and playing tricks on me, taking advantage of my obliviousness to many social cues. As I got older, verbal abuse graduated to physical abuse.

There was the time that a group of guys at school started calling me "wank," because at a sleep-over one of them interpreted the leg movement stim that helps me get to sleep (which I continue to do to this day, because, you know, it's a stim) as me inappropriately masturbating.

There was the time in my first year of high school when a bully from the year above cornered me in front of all the boys in our year levels at lunch time. As I kept telling him "I don't want to fight you," he kept punching me in the face, humiliating me in front of dozens of my peers. Going to my next class after that lunchbreak, I was breathing heavily but emotionally numb, my face glowing hot from the residual impact of the punches. I felt powerless and even worse, ashamed of that powerlessness and of losing face in public. Later that day, numbness gave way to sadness, which I internalised to keep up some sort of brave face.

There was the time at an Under 14's basketball tournament where a group of my teammates thought it would be funny to hold me down, pull my pants off and smear Deep Heat liniment over my genitals. Everyone there laughed at me. Even I tried to laugh if off to save face. But the truth is that this was sexual assault, and it has scarred me ever since.

Before it happened, I remember realising that something was about to go down, dudes glancing at me and whispering to each other under their breath. I remember feeling terrified as they cornered me on the bed and pinned me down by force, ripping my pants down. And I remember the total violation of their hands, smearing the ointment over my dick and balls. It hurt. Physically hurt. Deep Heat on your sex organs burns like hell. Everyone had a good laugh while I stood with my dick out in front of an air conditioner for the following two hours, but under my forced smile I was in actual pain. The air conditioner was the only thing available to cool the burns. It was humiliating being assaulted in that way in front of not just my team, but members of the girls' teams and the Under 16's teams as well. Worst of all, the manager just sat there and laughed. That motherfucker was meant to look after us and have our backs, but he was just part of the mob. I've never felt so alone as I did at that moment.

At so many stages growing up, people around me seemed to be more in tune with my difference than I was, and because I was different, I could be the object of their "fun." I couldn't say it then, so I'll say it now: I never consented to be that object and that shit was never acceptable. They may say that it was just a joke, but I can assure you I was never laughing. I will not be the punchline in anybody's joke.

WEARING MASKS

That feeling of being trapped behind enemy lines in hostile territory never goes away. I've worn many different masks as survival adaptations in hostile environments. I didn't begin masking con-sciously, they just evolved as unconscious survival adaptations.

The mask I've most commonly worn as an adult is related to my profession: I'll call it the "quintessential academic."

In my mind, as I progressed through the ranks of academe, the "quintessential academic" is a font of knowledge and wisdom, who can monologue off-the-cuff with great eloquence, in any setting. They have a commanding presence and project an air of confidence, of having everything under control, of being totally "boss." They are respected public figures who cultivate their own media "brand" and are well-connected with a network of colleagues across aca-demia, media, government, and business. They are worldly and well-travelled, with tales of exciting overseas exploits, who win large grants and booze up at conferences. "Philosopher-king" would be a bit much, but not far off, in my imagination of the quintessential academic.

Clearly this is a ridiculous caricature and a stupid fucking mask to want to wear, but it's a mask I've ended up wearing to hide feel-ing like an impostor in academia, never quite measuring up. It was this mask that I was wearing during the TV interview, it was this caricature that I was trying to project myself as to the world. But masks have a finite energetic shelf life and under too much stress, as was clear in that interview, they crumble.

Wearing the "quintessential academic" mask, I'm playing a role that has a predictable shape and trajectory. As an academic, being a semi-public figure provides a structure to inter-personal interactions that makes it easier for me to converse with others. People know who I am, even if I don't know them, and that pro-vides a more predictable framework to how we interrelate that's less stressful for me. When people come to me, it circumvents the crippling discomfort I feel at initiating interactions.

But beyond its social utility, wearing the "quintessential academic" mask is impossible to sustain under real-world stresses. While on an academic tour to North Korea in 2012, a famous American professor asked me what I was listening to on my headphones during a long bus ride from Pyongyang to Wonsan.

"MP3 player," I mumbled back. Fuck. Way to be the "philosopher-king" Ben! But on reflection, this moment was entirely predictable: I was tired, ambushed with a conversation I hadn't primed for, in a noisy bus, surrounded by senior academic colleagues I was wildly intimidated by, while trying to take in every detail of the unique landscapes we were driving through.

Take academic conferences as another example. While not quite North Korea, I still find it difficult to wear the "quintessential academic" mask in those environments. At my first ever conference presentation in 2007, my panel was the first of the morning and having not been to a conference before I had no idea how these events worked. I was the first speaker on the panel. After I concluded my presentation, I packed up my notes and left the room, to bewildered looks from the audience. I didn't realise that panel presentations usually conclude with a Q&A session. Buzzing with anxiety, I was just happy to get out of the room.

At another conference the following year I had the dreaded experience of cramming a forty-minute presentation into a fifteen-minute presentation slot. By the ten-minute mark it was clear I had way too much material to cover. My body started to heat up and my brow began to bead with sweat. When the panel chair signalled "two minutes remaining," I started to get the mental blanks and lose my place in my notes. I got through but danced perilously close to a full-blown anxiety spiral.

As recently as last year, I was panel chair in the final session of an international relations conference. It was the end of the day and I was physically and emotionally spent after spending a full two days of "people-ing" and presenting my own paper earlier in the day. On not one, but two occasions, I got the titles of the presentations mixed up when introducing the speakers, then struggled to facilitate the Q&A at the back end of the session. I tried to pass it off with humour, but I felt unprofessional and that I'd let me colleagues down. I was so drained from human interaction that my executive function was compromised, but prior to my autism diagnosis I didn't have a frame of reference for that experience that didn't involve personal failure.

Academia is an elite profession and performance pressure goes with the territory. But within this context, juggling the competing demands of high-level research, large teaching loads, community service, administrative duties, and compliance with often nonsensical bureaucratic processes presents unsustainable multi-tasking challenges that are hostile to my autistic brain. This is not helped by perpetual organisational change and insecurity of employment, which takes an enormous toll on the psychological well-being of academics. I wore the mask of the "quintessential academic" to survive in this environment, but I could only wear it for so long until something gave way.

But the most pernicious aspect of this is that the incentive structures of academic labour favour the "quintessential academic." My profession wants me to wear that mask. Sorry academia, it's not me, it's definitely you.

When the "quintessential academic" façade crumbles, I've always got the "funny guy" mask to fall back on. Indeed, a razor-sharp wit has been my Swiss army knife of coping strategies.

I suspect I first developed humour as a mask to deflect bullying when I was in primary school and refined the art as I moved into high school. As a non-aggressive, highly sensitive kid, I saw returning verbal fire as my only pro-active defence against the people who would try to pick on me.

I would use humour in an attempt to laugh off taunts which in reality were cutting me deeply inside. But my razor-sharp wit had a forked tongue. I'd use that wit to cut down others to make myself feel better, externalising my frustrations as an unconscious outlet. I would lash out in situations where I felt out of control and emotionally maxed out, what I now recognise as a form of autistic meltdown. This would land me in trouble and make me feel even worse about myself, triggering a shame spiral that had depression as its end point.

As an adult I have deployed humour to deflect attention in situations where I feel anxious and uncomfortable. *Don't get me wrong, there are moments when I am genuinely funny, but hiding behind the "funny man" mask is a reflex, an adaptive crutch that traps me in superficial interactions and compels me to make stupid comments that don't do justice to my depth of thought.*

I often reflexively fall back on the "funny man" mask in academic professional settings now, particularly at the times when I feel so overwhelmed that even "quintessential academic" mask is untenable.

Another mask I've worn is the "party boy." It started when I was eleven years old, when I decided to get into trouble more at school as a means of becoming more popular. I had discovered that demonstrating intelligence and being nice was not an effective pathway to social acceptance. Instead, I chose the attention-seeking tactic of trying to be bad-ass and doing stupid shit to get social approval, a tactic that worked often enough for me to internalise it.

That approval was like an addictive drug for my teenage mind, particularly when alcohol became part of the mix in my mid-teens. I remember the first time I got drunk, with a group of friends after an end-of-year social in Year Ten. The feeling of being part of the group was just as intoxicating as the nasty mix of cheap whiskey, vodka, and cola I was drinking. We bonded through the process of engaging in something illicit and clandestine...it felt like I was being inducted into some secret society!

By the time I got to university I was thoroughly committed to wearing "party boy" as my mask of choice, through attention-seeking and alcohol. Coping with the sensory overload and the anxiety burden of living on campus in student accommodation, I engaged in self-destruction masquerading as social bonding as my survival strategy. Getting drunk 3-4 nights a week was common, as was blazing up trees of weed during the days in between. Sooner or later, I was convinced, I'd be socialised enough that the anxiety would dissolve away.

The "fun" of wearing "party boy" came at a cost: I completely failed my first year of university, acquired a beer belly that has been with me ever since, and carved a yawning hole in my soul which, because I didn't properly understand my neurology, prompted an existential crisis that took me the next fifteen years to figure out.

That's the cruel irony of my masks; each of them undercuts the others, leaving an unfillable hole. As I began to consciously embrace my madness, I've asked myself who I really am without the masks. "What's my defence mechanisms and what's the real me? Who the fuck am I?" Having no clear answer to that question has been deeply disorienting.

SENSORY ENVIRONMENTS

I honestly thought that I was just shy and that my anxiety would just fade away once I'd had enough social experience. From that standpoint, it's clear to see why alcohol was so seductive in my late teens. Being drunk dulled my anxiety and allowed me to step outside of my comfort zone, and the space to step out of my head enough to connect with other people.

This is also what led me to experiment with ecstasy in the rave scene. Unlike alcohol, which is a depressant drug, ecstasy is a stimulant that promoted feelings of euphoria and overwhelming empathy with other people, along with the ability to engage in the amazing kinetic release of dancing all night to hard music.

My first outdoor rave was a revelation; dancing under the clear night sky of early summer in the Adelaide Hills, dancing to hard trance beats with a rhythm and purpose I never knew I possessed, hugging my friends, and feeling part of something full of love and positivity. I'd never felt anything remotely that powerful before.

But the power of the connection and release of the ecstasy high was only temporary, and it couldn't make me feel better all the time.

One night of partying on the weekend would conclude with several days of comedown and recovery, building up to reaching for the high again the following weekend. This was a treadmill, a weekly cycle of physical and emotional recovery from the last party, while preparing for the next one. What started out as liberation ended up as self-destruction, leading to recurrences of the depression that I was attempting to escape. No matter how much "social experience" I had, the anxiety would never go away.

Pubs, clubs, and music festivals were where the people and the music were happening, and that's where I thought I had to be. Because of my neurology the only way I could be in those environments without immense discomfort was to be blind drunk or three pills down.

Without the aid of alcohol and stimulants, I run out of energy quickly in large-group social situations. I wear these masks to cope but can't escape the nagging feeling that I am being inauthentic (while desperately not wanting to be). There are other times when I pull out of social engagements at the last minute because I just don't have the energy it takes to interact.

With the loneliness of social withdrawal came shame and guilt, hyper self-criticisms such as "I am letting other people down," "people hate me," "I am missing out on life and it's my fault," "I am selfish," "I am a bad person" ...and on and on the self-hatred goes. By this stage of the descent, I would be left numb, as if the ability to feel any positive emotion was lost. I now understand that I'd been trying to socialise in inhospitable neurotypical environmental niches that were slowly destroying me.

EPILOGUE

I'm an International Relations specialist, not a scholar of Madness or Neurodiversity. But I am an expert on myself and my own lived experience of madness and neurodivergence. I've obviously been autistic all my life; however, my journey into conscious understanding and integration of this reality is still relatively recent.

Through this chapter I've reflected on how my moment of infamy on live TV, my "nuclear meltdown," became a moment of transmutation, a catalysing event that led me to "come out" twice, as Mad, and then as autistic.

I am indebted to everyone who has come before me in the Madness and Neurodiversity movements who have helped chart the map that I'm following in my journey. I hope that in coming out (twice), my story adds another small data point to our map, to help the people who come after us on their own journeys of self-understanding and liberation, and to find community and acceptance for who we are.

killing the mood:
a bi-vocal commentary
on bipolar humor

LEAH HEILIG AND BAILEY S. KIRBY

For two late greats, and the source of some tattoos, Carrie Fisher & Peter Mayhew

It's day seven. Biblically: a day of rest and completion. For SSRI withdrawal: barfing up some Paxil in the shopping cart bay of a JOANN Fabrics.

"Oh god," I mutter as an encore to some of my $6 macchiato coming up from that morning.

"I told you to stay the fuck home," I think god would have said in return.

Mariah Carey's "All I Want for Christmas Is You" plays in the background.

———

I originally came to JOANN to buy something for a creative outlet. My therapist suggested it, and I have what used to be called Van Gogh's Disease, so I figured I better start learning to express myself through landscapes. Except I don't know shit about crafting, so my entire trip has comprised me squinting through lights that are too yellow, being nauseated at air that smells like too much pinecone, and wearing what I'm going through all over my body: a ratty beanie over greasy hair, unwashed and saggy jeans, smeared glasses, and a 20-year-old sweatshirt with the collar stretched out beyond reason or repair.

I also don't know how to *shop* for crafts, so before The Barfening, I just wander from bin to bin, bobbing like a slowly deflating balloon, until I stop at one full of yarn skeins. As part of not knowing shit about crafting, I don't know shit about yarn, so I just kind of hold it in a critical way. For therapy.

Ah, I think. This one feels like it weighs $6.99. Good heft. Good absorption for the sour sweat trying to ooze out of my palms. It's also blue. For therapy.

"Do you need help?" asks someone in a red apron, possibly because she saw I was holding yarn like a call for...well. Therapy.

"Yes," I say, not buying anything.

After the barf, I'm politely but firmly ushered out the door like the smelly trash I am. Lots of guilt, no therapy, no landscapes.

I get in my truck, slowly pull off my beanie, wipe my mouth on my already dirty sleeve, and am kind of bummed about the waste of a good Starbucks gift card on top of my exit from civilized society.

———

When I tell the story later—*years* later—I don't expect laughs, exactly, but I definitely don't expect it to hang in the room until it's absorbed by the nearest flat surface, until people feel like they can wait it out long enough to change the subject. I don't expect to snuff the life out of the party when I say I have proof I can't stomach a poor Merino wool. I've since learned that what I get to say about my life has the same constraints as a 1950s housewife adding olives to the Jello recipe to save a disaster of a dinner party: I can't leave a bad taste in anyone's mouth (or mine, apparently) or it's over.

As a Mad person, I'm allowed to tell jokes—stories—but only in the right ways. There's rules, you see. Like no using the B word ("Bipolar" is reserved for kitschy pop songs or edgy keychains or unpredictable friends) and nothing about hygiene (you can be a messy bitch, but god help you if you're a depressed and smelly one). You also have to be a little bit miserable the whole time you're talking about it, full of that unspoken obligation to society at large to suffer tragically from Madness instead of laughing with it.

Well, fuck all that. Let's celebrate the jokes that don't land.

We (turns out there's been two of us Bipolars this whole time) have decided to share some stories where our sense of humor troubles the boundaries of what's acceptable. Sometimes it's uncomfortable (for us and maybe for you), and sometimes it's hilarious (for us and maybe not for you). And sometimes there's the unpalatability of olives and Jello, but that's just because it pairs well with depressive drinking.

BI-VOCAL STORYTELLING: A NOTE ON STYLE

So right now, we could step up to the podium and Educate. Tell you how Bipolar is like at the optometrist: there's a type 1, a blink, and a type 2—one more in focus than the other for each of us. But instead, we want to throw the podium out the window. You'll notice that we haven't identified ourselves individually yet—and for the rest of this chapter, we won't. It doesn't matter if you know whose voice you're hearing, whose story you're reading. We want to trouble the expectations of "I" and "we" in the same ways that we trouble what's funny.

We've known each other for six years, over half that time with coordinating Bipolar diagnoses, like a left and right shoe. Sometimes one of us is depressed and can't read, one of us is manic and can't sit still, or we're both running on three hours of sleep and can't see straight. On those days, we play hot potato with our brains:

"I'll write this section and you yell at me about it until it's right."

"Hey, where the fuck did I put that fucking book yesterday?"

"Help me with this email and I'll schedule your haircut."

"It's 3 p.m. and all I've had since 5 is two cups of coffee and a mug of expired oatmeal. What's for lunch?"

It's all just 1 potato, 2 potato, 3 potato, 4. That's how we wrote these stories, and that's how we're going to present them to you: through this fractured and messy means of bi-vocal storytelling that blends our experiences of mania, depression, and mixed cycles into, well, a bunch of uncomfortable jokes. Ten, to be exact. They're disjointed and irreverent and probably as tough to read as they were to write. But we invite you to lean into your discomfort or your eye rolls, to notice the moments when you write us off or skip ahead.

We want to kill the mood.

UPPERS AND DOWNERS

Here is how my time will go, for a little bit, while time lasts.

I'm going to learn Spanish and knit and watch the entirety of Akira Kurosawa's filmography to become a movie critic right this second because otherwise the concept of film itself is going to run out. Afterwards, I will wake up (maybe, if I sleep) like some kind of shitty werewolf who doesn't remember the night before. Duolingo will be installed and perpetually asking me to say pants, there will be a box full of yarn in every room of the house (for pursuing the perfection of the purl stitch at 4 a.m., not for roping together red strings of conspiracy on a bulletin board while chain smoking over them. Although sometimes I do do that. But it's only because I'm an academic by trade and I get paid to do it if I call them litera-ture reviews.), and I will have Cask-of-Amontillado'd my own ass in black-and-white box sets. I may have to Jenga money between accounts to pay the credit card bill, but I will sure as shit be able to tell you what parts of *The Last Jedi* were an homage to *Rashōmon*.

I will then deep clean my entire house. This will delight the peo-ple around me, because I have not done so for about two months. I will make sure that handles on things are spotless, that the wall has the dirty parts of paint scraped off by my thumbnail. Then I will pick out the dirty skin around the nail. I will wake you up at 4 a.m. to tell you about pantalones, and everything will fall into place. One, twothree. I'll be going fast but it won't matter because everything lines up even if it means that I throw out half your stuff and reorganize half of mine in the space it frees up. For projects, or whatever.

People who don't understand ask, "How do you get so much done in a day?"

I'm supposed to say, "[deprecating or humble statement]"
They say, "I'm jealous."

I've started to say, "Well I don't sleep anymore."
They laugh and clear their throats.

Not my best material, they'll just have to find it funny later. But the joke makes sense to me. Because I'm a fucking helium balloon with a bottle of Pledge.
UpUpAway
LiveLaughLove
ManiacManiacCleaningFloors

1: BIPOLAR HUMOR IS ABOUT THE CAPTIVE AUDIENCE.

———

Now I'm a puddle of goop on the couch, nesting in a pile of blankets with my hair getting greasier by the day. Last week's unfinished projects cover every flat surface like little mountains of accusations. Can't wait to see how many meetings and social obligations Manic Me scheduled in a flurry of aspiration. I'll back out of them all. I'm always cleaning up after that optimistic asshole.

The optimism can sometimes pay off, I concede as I shuffle to the kitchen to prepare my one meal of the day. The freezer is packed with shitty stoner food and dumplings. I prepared for the apocalypse this time. As close as I get to #selfcare.

My partner comes home from work, bringing a flurry of stories from the day and a level of energy I should envy. Instead it just makes me angry. I burrow further into my fluffy cave, emerging ever so often to grumpily pick at a plate of room-temperature dinosaur-shaped chicken nuggets.

This cave, and its surroundings, is a depression den. But it's more than a place. It's a way of life that imparts a unique ability to ignore terrible things that would require effort—any effort—to fix. Oh, the pile of recyclables is almost as tall as me? The living room is 50% composed of paper plates littered with half-eaten pizza crusts? I haven't showered in 4 days? Never noticed. No idea what you're talking about.

If a regular ol' depression den has a low bar, a Bipolar depression den has an even *lower* bar. There's always something in the back of my mind saying, "It's okay, you'll be manic eventually, the mess doesn't matter." Even if it takes another six months, that's Manic Me's problem. Hopefully she'll show up soon; I have ten unfinished beverages on my desk, and that's perilously close to a personal best and an intervention.

Sometimes I forget that not everyone lives this way.

As I ripped the head off of the last chicken stegosaurus on that sunny, miserable afternoon, my co-worker came by with a Christmas gift. Before she got to my house, she texted to ask where to put the bag.

I just said, "Drop it off by the rotting jack-o'-lanterns :)"

She never replied.

2: BIPOLAR HUMOR IS LEAVING SHIT TO ROT.

———

Once I had a horrible time sleeping for several months straight. I would lie in bed for hours, staring at the ceiling, buzzing under every inch of my skin, unwilling to move to the couch because one tiny cockroach had crawled on me there in the middle of the night a year prior and I couldn't not listen for its little feet scraping against a baseboard (yes, that's a thing) or see its little shadow fall on the floor and I couldn't get up from the bed anyway because what if standing took my attention away from keeping myself from bursting at the seams and what if my racing thoughts fell out and I could never think again. Eventually I begged my psychiatrist for a medication that would help me sleep. I swore I wasn't manic.

The first attempt was Remeron. I took half a pill the night before my birthday and was so out of it the next day that I have no memory of how we celebrated. I do kind of remember sitting at a baseball game and trying to figure out why everyone looked so far away. The next time I talked to my psych, I asked her if the meds were supposed to make me feel like I was watching Earth all the way from Mars.

"I...don't know what that means. How much did you take?"

"Half a pill. And it *means* that I slept and was probably body-snatched in the process. But actually it's fine because maybe this body is a little stronger." I laughed at the prospect, flexing one arm for effect.

She scribbled on my chart and ignored the quip.

"You didn't listen to me when I prescribed this. A half pill is stronger for adults than a whole pill would be." She added something about it being a children's antidepressant and the dosage being tuned to their weird little metabolisms.

"HOW does that make ANY sense? And WHY do they prescribe this shit to CHILDREN?"

"Just try it."

I guess the adult dose doesn't summon the aliens, because I'm pretty sure I wasn't body-snatched again. It also didn't help me sleep, which I suppose is more important. But I kept the Remeron. Just in case.

3: BIPOLAR HUMOR IS AN OUT-OF-BODY EXPERIENCE.

———

My fatalistic sense of humor usually manifests itself in joking about being other things in a self-deprecating manner. Guess I'll just be dirt. Guess I'll go be garbage, that sort of thing. Once, after sitting on the steps of my back porch and feeling my heart thud too much, I texted a friend—one who is not Mad or at least one who hides it better than I do—that I might as well go be a tree.

I don't remember the exact wording, but it boiled down to them asking if I needed someone to come over. To intervene in my turning a new leaf. I was unaware at the time (and still don't understand) that the desire to go green would be interpreted as a call for help. I always imagined that if I chose to make one it would be more drastic: on the top of a building, standing in the cold rain—at the very least, there'd be a mixtape and more cigarettes involved. But apparently it was wanting to reduce, reuse, recycle that sent up red (green?) flags.

I said no thanks to the kind offer because (1) I thought I was just making a joke (albeit a weird one), and (2) I was living in a downswing. At that point, no amount of interest in my well-being is an equivalent exchange for washing dishes. The exhaustion is too heavy, *and* I have to explain my sense of humor before scrambling to find some scented candles and dignity? No no. Sane guests have to operate on vampire rules when it comes to Mad houses: they can stop by, but they can't go in without an invitation.

Still, some do.

One time, I was home alone and on too little sleep and too much anxiety. I heard the crackle of the radio on the floor below me, murmuring, and was convinced that emergency services were going through my things and searching my home. For what, I don't remember.

What I do remember are three feelings:

Terror: I thought they had come because I had done something wrong. I thought they were there to take my dogs away.

Embarrassment: Why hadn't I done the fucking dishes? I had company over.

Annoyance: They weren't abiding by the vampire rules.

They weren't real, turns out. But I hadn't really called for their help, so fair's fair.

I promise to the world at large: I will not be a tree if you promise to text me at least 3 days in advance of any home visit.

4: Bipolar humor is a weird sort of hospitality.

———

In my mid-ish 20s, I was on medications that treated anxiety and depression. One was Klonopin and the other was Paxil. The former made me drool and the latter made me want to die, which didn't work.

I have non-memories of Klonopin—things I did that other people remember for me, because my head was not unlike the cotton used to cushion the pills in their bottle. Apparently some of these non-memories are hilarious. The punchline is still there, even if

I'm not the one always telling it. One such memory involves a Bipolar's paradise: Target.

It's a story that needs some serious Hot Potato Brain, so let's go.

1 Potato.

Wandering through Target with no objective was a common activity for me and my fellow Depressives at the time, since we lived in Lubbock, Texas, and there wasn't much else to do. It also fed my mania, what with the infinite opportunities for extravagant spending on items I would never see again. On this particular day, I did have one specific thing on my list: dryer sheets.

We circled the clothing section, meandered through the baby stuff (why? we had no babies. but wait, was I drooling? the Klonopin must have kicked in.), picked up a smattering of junk food to go with the Kurosawa marathon I never had. With every step, my panic ballooned. I knew—I just knew!—that if I didn't get dryer sheets immediately then I would never have the opportunity to get them. They would no longer exist. Nothing would dry again.

2 Potato.

Suddenly I was in the laundry aisle, which felt more like a twisting hall of mirrors with each passing second, my objective getting farther and farther out of my reach. Wait, what are dryer sheets, again? Not literally, but more philosophically: why did I need them, why did anyone need them? Did I write them down only to ask myself this later?

My friend stepped between me and the looming towers of products, grabbing one off the shelf.

"Here, let's go."

I stared at the box, petted it, wondered why it wasn't soft. There was supposed to be a window here that let you see into the reality—instead there's only a two-dimensional bear. Aren't dryer sheets soft? Were all the real dryer sheets gone because I was too late? Guilt plagued me.

3 Potato.

As we turned to leave, I ran straight into an open-mouthed 18-year-old. I mumbled something about dryer sheets and wiped the drool off my chin (I assume). My friend held it together until we got to the register and then cracked up: "That was one of my students, and I am going to hear about this tomorrow." I was too busy cradling my box to care. This box of potential lies and disappointment.

4.

I never did laundry. Instead I fell asleep on the kitchen floor for three months.

5: BIPOLAR HUMOR IS KNOWING NOT WHAT I DO.

———

Scene: A campfire party, complete with strangled renditions of "Friends in Low Places" and "Wagon Wheel," a passed-around bottle of god-knows-what, and a cloud of smoke that carries notes of tobacco and weed.

Someone I don't know asks the group, "How do you think you'll die?"

My mania responds instantly: "Walking out in front of a car."

I would say you could've cut the tension with a knife, but I don't think they make a blade sharp enough.

I try to salvage the moment: "It doesn't require math!"

The fire dies with the joke.

6: BIPOLAR HUMOR IS DEADPAN.

———

I'm really bad at naming my emotions, and I'm cool with that. It keeps me alive. Here's my logic: If I've been depressed for a couple months, I'm probably about to go on a manic bender. Or vice versa. My brain has to figure out how to keep my crazy ass from ruining my life in one way or another next week, so knowing what I'm feeling at any given moment is the least of its concerns. I just accept that instead of consistent emotional regulation, I'm going to have a mini-breakdown once or twice a year. For a weekend, I get to process 6-12 months of shit, cry like my life depends on it, eat basically nothing, and make my partner wonder if I'm dying. But then I feel great. 10/10 can recommend dealing with all your shit at once. Makes everyday life a lot more bearable.

See, when you're saving up for a breakdown, everything carries the same level of importance. Everything is fine, everything is terrible, and everything is hilarious. But again, sometimes I forget that other people don't live like this. Sometimes I learn that the hard way.

A couple years ago I drove to Asheville, North Carolina, for a one-night trip. I hated traveling by myself, but for once I thought it might be okay.

I was very wrong. And it was the fucking pizza scissors that did me in.

My Airbnb basement apartment had two cursed doors. The first was at the top of a set of stairs that descended into the middle of the room. It had no visible lock and guarded the switch for half the lights in the place. I opted to survive in partial darkness. The second door made the first one look like the entrance to Disneyland. It had a deadbolt, a chain, a padlock, and a ragged bottom edge designed for fingers and ghosts and who knows what else to creep out of. While offering a video tour to a friend, I made the obvious joke that the apartment was kind of like a physical representation of my brain: shadowy corners and several rooms best left unexplored. She suggested I go back home. I just laughed. And wondered what I might have in common with whatever they were keeping down there.

After settling in the best I could, I left my 5-star personal gateway-to-hell in favor of downtown. I wandered the streets, took in the sights, wished North Carolina had a more lenient open container law. I had my first-ever anxiety attack in my car and then went to get pizza.

I hit up a brewery with a dizzying collection of sours—my favorite—and ordered dinner. I took the last open table—"open" being the operative word. It was right in front of the bar and more conspicuous than I'd prefer, but in Beer City on a Friday night you take what you can get. The "personal pizza" I ordered came out as a deep dish rectangle longer than my forearm, unsliced and accompanied only by an imposing pair of angled utility scissors arranged artfully on the charcuterie board someone classier than me decided would set the right mood. As drunken strangers pressed past me, gawking and holding empty glasses high, I hacked at that pizza like I was an angry kindergartener forced to make a shitty Mother's Day card in art class.

When I returned to the basement, its horrors were overshadowed by those fucking scissors. I couldn't stop thinking about them. Someone had a really twisted sense of humor. And *I'm* the one they call insane.

Afterward, I told the rest of this story to the friend who had told me to come home. She was immediately appalled.

"I'm sorry, wait, you had an *anxiety attack*, and what you want to tell me about is pizza scissors?!"

7: BIPOLAR HUMOR IS HAVING YOUR PRIORITIES IN ORDER.

————

When it's 3 a.m. and I can't sleep, the golden arches are pretty reliable for some human interaction when you need that sort of thing. There's a song by Electric Six called "Down at McDonaldz," where I think the meaning is just getting drunk in its parking lot and the chorus is "People need a place to go!" repeated. You have to have a certain mindset (Insomnia? Alcoholism? Troubled™?) for that to resonate, but it does in my case because when you go four or five or ten nights with these hours you want to remember people exist. Or that you exist. There's a liminal space between insomnia and fast food that is very tangible. I go to get a coke through the drive-thru.

I hit the first window.

"Is that a Chewbacca on your neck?"

"Uh."

Sometimes I forget about it, but the tattoo's a figurative albatross and a leftover. Almost all my tattoos are leftovers, 30-minute decisions.

"THIS CHICK'S GOT A CHEWBACCA ON HER!"

I go to the next window. Three people are there and now the liminal space is existential. Am I embarrassed or cool or a trash fire?

"Let's see the Chewbacca!" one asks, and this is now a comedy of errors.

I crane my neck. It's a $25 tattoo that looks so much like $25 I'm kind of amazed they recognize what it's supposed to be from that distance.

"YEAH, THAT'S A CHEWBACCA!"

"Yeah," I agree.

"IS THAT A TATTOO?"

"Yeah," I agree again.

Since then it's a default answer.

"What's an interesting fact about yourself?"

"Chewbacca neck tattoo."

"What'd you do over break?"

"Chewbacca neck tattoo."

"Describe yourself in three words."

"Chewbacca neck tattoo."

"How have you been adjusting to your new meds?"

"Chewbacca neck tattoo."

8: BIPOLAR HUMOR IS CHEWBACCA NECK TATTOO.

———

Some people say the two flavors of Bipolar are different disorders, and others say they're the same damn thing. I don't really care which is true, all I know is that my Bipolar is like a box of chocolates. The bane of my existence is not mania, the part that can ruin me financially. It's not even depression, the part that can kill me. It's the part where I never know what I'm gonna get—the so-called mixed episodes unique to Bipolar 2. When I'm depressed with high mental energy that feels like incessant buzzing under the skin of my motionless body. When I'm Doing All The Things and really fucking sad about it. When it is my literal bane, because I have just enough energy to feel like I can make the misery end once and for all.

No matter the balance of the mix, I can't do a fucking thing I'm supposed to do. But I *can* swan around the house drag-queen style instead of just pacing, elevate my depressive drinking from straight vodka to a chocolate martini (no olive, unless the mania is strong with this one), and create ridiculous musical mashups in my brain.

[enter, pursued by foghorn] Hey everybody, I'm DJ Mixed!!!

Say hello to a truly bizarre side effect of my Bipolar. Two songs will just *appear*, seamlessly intertwined, in my brain. Without asking permission first. Sounds annoying as fuck, but I've become quite fond of it. One time I even got three songs, but I can't for the life of me remember what they were.

In 2018 I started a playlist to immortalize my creations. Listening to each of the two songs one after the other—or in alternating chunks, for bonus points—will really put you in a Bipolar state of mind. Gotta especially recommend the first, third, and fifth pairs.

"My Humps," Black Eyed Peas
"Hey Mickey," Toni Basil

"Tearin' Up My Heart," N•Sync

"Love on Top," Beyoncé

"I Think We're Alone Now," Tiffany
"Dancing on My Own," Robyn

"We Didn't Start the Fire," Billy Joel
"1985," Bowling for Soup

"Toxic," Britney Spears
"Your Body Is a Wonderland," John Mayer

"Return to Sender," Elvis Presley
"These Boots are Made for Walkin'," Nancy Sinatra

When I bring this up—it's a great party trick—people are fascinated but with an undercurrent of awkwardness. My brain on its mixed bullshit is the poster child for Mad creativity gone a little too weird. I'm supposed to paint my feelings or write the next great American novel before sticking my head in an oven. No one ever said anything about involuntary hybrid earworms. And no one's really sure if they're allowed to laugh. Is it tragic? Is it even real? What does it have to do with Bipolar?

Here's what I've realized: mashing up songs gives my brain something to chew on so it doesn't chew on itself. If feeling suicidal is the ultimate act of self-destruction, this shit is my brain's ultimate act of self-preservation. I guess it really fucking likes chocolate.

9: BIPOLAR HUMOR IS HAVING MIXED FEELINGS.

————

Being disordered makes everything and everyone around you very pro-graph: therapy, apps on your phone, your bank accounts. Pro-graph and pro-color coded. The trends and warning signs over time are made clear to you verbally, visually, and on the third notice in the mail. If you're doing good, the graph points make a flat line and are usually green. If you're not doing so hot, they're zigzagged ski slopes and frequently on the warm parts of the color wheel.

At one point in my life, all the graphs were in a certain range (high—to medium-risk) and all the pills came in the same color bottle. I was aggressively eating baby carrots in an effort to quit smoking, which I had started up again in an aggressive attempt to quit having panic attacks. My life was all a field in the same hue.

I have a terrier who's a good sport for all my post-therapy wind-down conversations. I remember sitting him down after a cigarette-carrot combo that was exactly as terrible as it sounds.

"I'm in my orange period," I informed him very seriously, like a docent.

I remember my dog putting his paw on my leg, as if to say: *you can't even paint.*

10: BIPOLAR HUMOR IS GETTING YOUR KICKS WHILE YOU'RE DOWN.

IN BAD TASTE: PARTING THOUGHTS ON MESSY SLEEVES

At the end of all this, we are left with a question: what does it mean to laugh Mad?

In the saneist world, there's trouble with the answer. Too much Mad laughter risks something. It comes at the wrong times, is directed at the wrong things. Because of the inability to translate, Mad humor gets perceived as something other than funny. Sometimes that's threat—where the discomfort crosses over the threshold into unnerving, and the unnerving into the saneist labels of unhinged or violent.

"I don't think I'm that angry," I said one time after leaving therapy, where it was suggested I try anger management, for being angry.

"To me you're always seething," replied a friend.

Maybe laughing Mad is about exhaling from the seethe.

Sometimes violence takes on a different shape, like we explored in this piece. It takes on the violence of willful misunderstanding, of frustration, of infantilizing. It comes across as awkward or un-relatable or cringey. When Bipolar becomes an act of storytelling, Bipolar also becomes a performance, and with that comes a new set of threats—ones even we create.

We could be, for example, enacting violence of our own by blanketing what Bipolar humor is when we know damn well how nuanced and variable the experience is. We are also aware of the entanglements our lives have formed with the psychiatric system, and the strife between it and Madness, Mad Pride, and anti-psy-chiatry movements. But as Mad, Bipolar women living in a world primed for violence against us because of it, we have to be authen-tic to all elements of our stories, which at this point includes med-ication. We're cognizant of the fact that we're defining the Bipolar experience narrowly, according to only two perspectives that have happened to find a particular brand of humor in the circumstances.

So, why *do* we find Bipolar hilarious? Is it because it's dark, a response to said violence?

Maybe, but leaving it there's too simple. We reject the saneist notion of Mad humor as *just* a coping mechanism. There's a unique happiness inherent in mood killing, in embracing the sad trom-bones and finding joy in the discomfort. In sharing these stories, we had to let Bipolar take the wheel and drive us off the nearest cliff as it has done before and will do again. To let it be a partner in crime instead of an arresting officer. To have *fun* stirring olives into Jello and serving it with a shit-eating grin. One of the most ubiquitous, silent acts of violence against Mad people is expecting us to pass through saneist expectations without disruption and without laughter, and our bi-vocal stories are an attempt to find both. We wanted, for a little while, to wear the unpalatable mess on our sleeves.

Speaking of wearing things on our sleeves.

We'd be remiss to have a piece on Bipolar and humor and not mention the late Bipolar icon Carrie Fisher, known to many as Princess Leia in the *Star Wars* movies.

You see, there's one more thing you should know about us. We have matching finger tattoos: a single parenthesis with one colon on each side. It's a symbol for Bipolar in certain (semi)circles, simultaneously a happy face and a sad face. Oversimplified maybe, but it works for us and many others. Having a Bipolar symbol permanently inscribed on our middle fingers, where it's obvious unless we intentionally hide it, can be both an inside joke that gets us through a rough day and a random spark that leads to productive conversation about Madness.

The tattoo placement is itself uncomfortable, inspired by Carrie Fisher's favorite brand of physical humor. She famously flipped off *Star Wars* director George Lucas during his American Film Institute Life Achievement Award acceptance speech in 2005, and then, until her death in 2016, hardly a photo op passed without her giving the one-finger salute. We now daily salute her.

This tattoo is so many things. It's pride in our Bipolar selves, a memory of a national treasure living loud, a source of laughter, and, sometimes, a warning to the sane among us: we aren't afraid to joke about even the dark side of Bipolar, and we especially aren't afraid of causing discomfort in the process.

Ultimately, for us, it's a reminder to live our lives the way Carrie Fisher would have wanted us to: irreverent and full of pills.

If all else fails, Bipolar humor is flipping the bird.

a perfect graveyard of buried hopes

(L.M. Montgomery, *Anne of Green Gables*)

MONICA K. SHIELDS

I woke in the dark. It was always dark. The stars were always out. It was always just me. The walls were curved, cool to the touch, textured. The mattress was wobbly and too soft and moved when I shifted my weight. The room had two exits. One, a door. The other, an open window. The buzzing and chirping of the jungle frogs they call coquí, the clicking and popping of night life, and the warm moist tropical air were unmistakable. I was in the jungle.

Like most things from this time, the space was oddly familiar but completely foreign. Fear, hunger, confusion were alive, living in my body. They wanted me to stay put, to cry. I had no idea where I was, when I was, why I was alone, why I was in the jungle.

Throughout my life, I could never let go of of the notion that I was completely unlovable. Now, I assumed I had finally been cast off somehow, by someone I didn't even know. I was truly fucked— trapped between my thoughts and survival. Confusion wrapped around and through my body, making me painfully aware of the fear that overtook my brain. The muscles of my face were sore from holding my eyes wide open. Dry stinging reminded me to blink. I held my breath tightly, in my abdomen, not released without intention.

I couldn't resolve the mismatch between my memories and what was in front of me. The clothes I wore, I had to admit, were something I'd own if I had no other style options. Still, they were impractical for the environment and my sensory needs. Oversized, thick basketball shorts with two layers of heavy fabric. A soft sports jersey with stitching and embellishments that made it rigid and scratchy. I should have been wearing things that that dried quickly. I like the compression of undergarments; I wasn't wearing any. I was filthy, covered in dirt. When I got a random whiff of myself, I smelled like I hadn't showered in years. I didn't recognize my shoes. They looked like they might belong to me, but mine were bright blue, newer; these were old, dingy, falling apart, brown. When I took a step, fluid squished between my toes. It seemed as if I had been wearing them, and nothing else, for years.

My body shuddered with sadness and despair, but no tears came. My body had always been my best friend, my guide, my protector; it held its own knowledge. It fed me with its reserves of fat. It soothed me when I was devastated from terrible thoughts.

Now, it held my soul through waves of tearless weeping. I began to realize that I couldn't trust my mind—it was unreliable. My body was all I had. Thinking made my head throb. I needed to listen to my body, to sleep. If I didn't, I'd crumple to the ground, hit my head (again), and fall asleep anyway.

I couldn't remember eating palmetto bugs (what the locals call cockroaches), geckos, lizards, and iguanas, but must have. I wondered how I was going to be able to put them in my mouth now that I realized what I had been eating. Everything was so dry. I wondered how long we had been in a drought.

My mind raced. there was no way to slow it down, or my body either. I sat or laid on that mattress, trying to rest, willing my body to walk the trail again. I watched my body. I let it be my guide—hunting for food, scanning for pools of water, avoiding tarantulas and other nighttime predators.

I was trapped in a loop of despair and sorrow. A loop of fear that only ended, it seemed to me, in literal death. Those fear loops, they were overwhelming, paralyzing. I sat on the ground, rocking, my knees pulled to my chest, my arms around my legs. The night sky, silhouettes of tall palm trees, and the moon held me, rocked me to sleep.

Mostly, I woke on the ground, sometimes on the mattress. Somehow, I didn't understand I was injured, even though I could feel large mats of blood and debris in my hair. There was a baseball-sized knot on my forehead and a bleeding wound on the back of my head. I had cuts, bruises, and open wounds on my limbs; I hurt all over. When I tried to figure things out, confusion would trigger a terrorscape in my mind, render me immobile. I had no idea how to think, to connect thoughts and make sense of them. I was aware of my body and thoughts but didn't understand what to do with them.

In the jungle, my mind didn't work. Thoughts wouldn't form; my mind was filled with holes. I watched thoughts grow and shatter. I could see images start to grow and then burst apart into tiny shards and scatter. I could see myself, but not feel myself. I didn't know how to exist. I didn't understand anything. I had to constantly remind myself to breathe and blink.

I tried to remember who or when I last engaged with someone. I knew I needed help but I didn't know what I needed. I collapsed from pain and woke up on the ground. My bladder felt tender; my bowels were full. I didn't know what these sensations meant or what to do with them. My lips were cracked; my mouth was dry. My stomach was swollen and firm. My limbs were stiff. My calf and hip muscles cramped.

Breathe and stack your parts. Move air in through the nose. Feet on the ground, ankles on top of feet, knees on top of ankles. Head up, shoulders back I walked and navigated the jungle until I was immobilized by fear or my body collapsed from exhaustion. I did this over and over again, for—so it seemed—years.

I did this all in darkness. Dark, always dark. Night? Perhaps.

One day, it started to get light; I could see where I was. The jungle. I recognized a house. Walked over. Went in. It looked abandoned. It wasn't. People were sleeping inside. Friends. My friends. But they were older. I was too tired to question why they were still there after the 40 years I'd been wandering in the jungle.

I lay down on a bed, on top of the covers. A friend was sleeping under the covers. I startled him.

In a few hours, an ambulance and some police showed up. Five men, all larger than me, all in full uniform, all speaking Spanish. They took turns staring into my eyes, as if examining my soul, looking for defects, unable to disguise their pity and disgust.

The compression from the seat belts on the stretcher in the back of the ambulance hugged my legs and hips, and my body relaxed into them.

I was brought, without my permission, to an emergency room in Puerto Rico, in a city about an hour from where I lived. I didn't know who I was, why I was in the hospital. I didn't have my cell phone or any personal belongings. I was held for observation, though I didn't know what that meant or why. I stayed there for several days. Frigid air-conditioned temperatures. Food I couldn't eat. Injected with medications I didn't want or need. Afraid of catching COVID. Staff didn't answer my questions. I didn't understand what was going on. I finally just—walked out.

I wore a shirt, an adult diaper, a pair of paper pants, and shoes. Only the shirt and shoes were mine. Two o'clock in the afternoon. I found myself near the back of the complex where the ambulances were parked. I walked around, trying to find an exit to the grounds. I hadn't had nearly enough water, exhausted, nothing to eat in days—or was it years?

I walked towards the busiest street, hoping it was the main road that traveled along the perimeter of the island. It wasn't. This short walk, maybe 5 blocks, exhausted me even more. I was aware of my exhaustion, aware that it was the hottest part of the day, the hottest part of the year. I didn't have much time or energy to make a wrong turn. I needed to get back to the city I lived in, where I was known by many, confident someone could get me to my apartment.

I didn't know which way to go. I walked towards the ocean. I was too far from where I lived to recognize the roads. The roads here didn't follow the coast like they did where I lived. Exhausted and hot, I needed to get out of the sun and think.

There was a small opening beside the road. A couple of concrete cement benches. A basketball hoop with no net. A few trees. The trees hid an opening that led under an overpass for a nearby road. I pushed aside vines and foliage to get through. I walked alongside a concrete embankment supporting the bridge. Protected from the elements, I was shielded from being seen by those driving by.

Two full sized pickup trucks might fit in the space if they could get there. Large rocks and tree limbs lay on top of dirt and gravel. I was the only one there, but I could see that others spent time in the area. Used syringes, empty bottles and cans, pieces of fabric, junk mail in piles. Empty takeout containers filled with ants, old sweatshirts stuffed into drain pipes. The walls were covered with new and old street art and graffiti. It didn't look a safe space for a single woman, but I didn't know where else to go.

I was on the west side of the island; the sun set around 6pm. I sat on an an almost-flat rock close to a concrete wall that I could lean against. As soon as I sat down, I felt my paper hospital pants rip. They were about 3 sizes too big, and the hole didn't expose my body, but it made me more insecure. The pants continued to get tears in them from my body's movement against the rock when I got up and down. I'd already removed the adult diaper, tossing it into a roadside garbage can; I was afraid these tears would expose my bare flesh.

The few hours before sunset went by fast. I couldn't figure out a way to get home. A very thin Puerto Rican man entered the space.

He wore dirty clothes, and a yellow knit cap on his head. His leg was wrapped in a bandage from ankle to knee. The bandage was dirty, too, and looked like it would cause more harm than good to whatever wounds it covered. He carried a plastic grocery bag, a package of doughnuts, a bottle of soda, and some takeout food from a food truck.

He said, "hola." I replied "hola," and looked nervously away. He said something in Spanish. I said, as I often did in such situations, "lo siento, mi Espanol mal" (I'm sorry, my Spanish is bad). He took a syringe and lighter out of his pocket and showed them to me. I looked at him, nodded, and looked away. While I watched circumspectly, the man unwrapped the bandage on his leg, used a can from the ground to heat something, then used the syringe to inject what he heated into his leg. Then he ate his food, drank his soda. He turned, looked at me, waved and smiled, and left, leaving his bag of trash.

I did not belong there. This was a bad spot to be in. The sun was setting, I didn't want to sleep there. I couldn't travel in an unknown area in the dark any better than during the day time. I knew that not all guys would be as non-threatening as he was. My mind spun with terror and the possibilities of what could happen to me if I stayed there. It was dark now. I was too afraid to leave. I got up from my rock every couple of minutes and walked around, over tree branches and through hanging vines, alongside the concrete embankment and out to the street. I looked around and came back. Seventy-five steps round trip. I did that circuit many times. I felt like a sitting duck if I didn't move, and I wanted to be familiar with the terrain in case I had to run.

After awhile I got sleepy, needed to find a way to rest. I used the rock I was sitting on as a pillow, and a torn piece of a store ad to cover the dirt on the ground. Sleeping outside, in the open, for the first time in my life. It felt like it might be my last night alive on this planet.

My fear turned to sadness. I didn't have a way to call my family or loved ones. Nobody I cared about knew where I was. Weak from exhaustion, confusion, dehydration, and malnourishment. I was in a very bad place, a place where people come to do things they don't want others to see. I thought about every terrible news story I had ever read. I remembered how close I was to the ocean, realizing how easily my body could be used, abused, and tossed into the water.

I didn't have the energy to cry. What would tears have done anyway? Only make me look more vulnerable. I didn't have the energy to fight off anyone. If I was attacked, I wouldn't fight back. There would be no point. This was it. It was my time to die.

I was angry with god. I had people that loved me and didn't understand me and would never understand me. I had someone I loved who would never know I felt. I had failed myself, those I loved, and those that loved me. I didn't understand how I got to this place, was certain I wouldn't make it through the night. I tried to make peace with my last night on Earth. I said a prayer to Gaia. I asked her to sooth my loved ones and let them know how much I loved them. I asked that whatever violence and harm came would be quick, so that I didn't realize what was happening when it occurred.

Dark night broke to light shades of blues and purples. I had made it through the night. Disappointment and discouragement filled me. I laid on the rock: what was the point of getting up? I watched the sky get bluer and bluer.

Another guy showed up. He, too, was thin, but he didn't have a bandage on his leg. Told me his name was Hector, asked for my name, in Spanish. He asked me if I had family, a husband, a mother, children. I said no, in poorly accented Spanish. He reached into a grocery bag, gave me an apple. He sat down a few feet away from where I lay, ate food, and did something with a syringe and lighter. This time I didn't watch.

He came over to me, and gave me his cap. He made the sign of the cross on his body, kissed his thumb, touched his forehead, then kissed his thumb again and reached out as if to touch my forehead. I stared at him with disbelief. What was happening? Was I being initiated into the street people? Was I being protected by a God that had forgotten me? I had no idea. He quickly left. I laid there, eating every available piece of apple, wearing the cap as a slight cushion between the rock and my head.

A short while later, he returned, this time with another guy. He looked like a street thug but talked like a cop. Spoke English. His name was Moses. I asked him if he was a cop and he said no, but sometimes he helps people who don't like the police. He asked me the same questions about family and why I was there. He asked if I would come with him to his outdoor restaurant. He said it was close by, had a toilet, some water. He said he had some errands to do, his wife needed him, but I should come with him because it wasn't safe there. He said I could figure out what to do at his restaurant and be safer than where I was at.

I got up and went. He was parked a few steps away; I got in the back seat and we drove a few miles to his restaurant.

He and Hector spoke in Spanish during the drive and at the restaurant. They were cleaning, doing food prep, not paying much attention to me. Except to bring baby wipes, hand sanitizer, bottles of water. I cleaned up as best I could. Asked if I could use his phone to look for friends on Facebook we might have in common so I could reach out for help.

He said, "Oh this is going to piss my wife off, but whatever," and handed me his phone.

I am a statistic.
Raised in poverty
and all that comes with that.
I have relationships with mental health institutions,
Debt.

Costs snowball and
Color every option
Their snowy white blanket creates a whiteout of options
Limits choices
Decisions made.
I am a statistic.

Generalized Anxiety. Severe Depression. Borderline Personality Disorder. Autoimmune. Cancer cells. Insomnia. Disorder.

Hello Satan

HELEN SILVERWOOD

The dazzling maestros at Tagenham Hospital were unable to find anything wrong with me, no matter how hard they tried. As long as I used their premeditated drugs, but abstained from all other mind-altering substances, I was odds-on favorite for success in a brave new life. They advised me that, in order to flourish in the community as an autistic person, I may need to try and avoid staring in the direction of other people whilst in deep contemplation. The recipients of my gaze would have no way of knowing it wasn't really them I was looking at. This could be unnerving for them to say the least, though it hopefully wouldn't alarm anyone enough to make them lash out at me. I may seem a bit odd to some people, but I'm certainly not any real danger to anyone—oh no, far from it. So, one fine Tagenham day, I was released from hospital, with strict instructions not to mix alcohol with my medication, as this could mean certain death.

Whether sane, insane, or just plain autistic, I was now ready to make a real good go of life in the community. I was on top of the moon about my newfound freedom. And what better way to springboard towards a new life than with the support of the wonderfully kind staff of the Young Person's Bristian Association hostel! So I gladly went and dossed down at the giant YPBA tower in Bromford, Hessex, trying to keep my nose clean while waiting for more permanent accommodation.

It was at the YPBA that I met Colin Casey, a person of apparent and utmost importance on the board of directors. He seemed safe enough, even blandly amiable. He wore steel-rimmed glasses as though they were an integral part of his shell pink face. His hair was neither blonde nor white, but rather the shade of dead cod that had been slowly stewed in a puddle of dirty water. As if to complete his harmless look, he had that familiar tuft of hair that always comes with a straw cropped bonce, whose owner doesn't take much care of it in the morning. Just a quick comb, then off to carry out his mission, with a vaguely nauseating smile that didn't look entirely genuine, though wasn't offensive either.

I'm sad to say it didn't take me long to become like an aggravated cobra when it came to the YPBA. Apart from a couple of wry sparkling car thieves, who at least had a sense of humour and plenty of enthusiasm, most YPBA residents were well into the process of surely and steadfastly losing their souls to a hollow consumerism and goodness knows what else, as far as I could see. After a few sickening but noneventful weeks, I felt like a blocked and infected abscess on one level. However I wasn't reacting further to this, either on the inside or the outside. I was so well-balanced that I was like a surfer on a tidal wave. I was confident that my medication wasn't necessary any more. I was absolutely fine! And, of course, if I didn't take it, I would be OK to have a drink if I felt like it! And I absolutely had begun to feel like it. I mean, most people drink don't they? It's not illegal. It can't be that bad, can it? So yes, I triumphantly weaned myself off my medication and started drinking again.

Over the next few months I came to clearly see why Bromford was also known as the capital of Babylon. I had gained in popularity since associating with criminals, scraping my hair into a ponytail and wearing Badidas t-shirts, but my heart was like a sunken fishing boat. The more I thought about it, the powers that be at the YPBA didn't exactly seem to be promoting a pure 'love thy neighbourhood' sort of Bristianity. I had my suspicions that they were practicing a false but powerful form of the religion; one which invoked Hell on earth, but with a façade of subtle but sickly niceness. Colin Casey in particular, was really beginning to grate on my raw nerves. I couldn't understand why everyone apart from me seemed to think that the sun shone out of every perforation in his body.

The YPBA residential community mostly consisted of sports-labeled teenagers from abusive homes, off the streets, or from recent vacations in drug rehabilitation centres and prisons. Colin Casey had given them a tower block over their heads, and was now teaching them about a power greater than themselves that could supposedly restore them to wellbeing. But, if you asked me, Mr Casey most definitely had a certain air about him that something was amiss. One time I was playing some lovely piano duets up in the music room with one of my favorite drinking acquaintances, the notorious alloy joyrider Nathorias Nickiboodle (Nat). I'm sure the tunes we were playing would have pulled on anyone's heart strings. Nevertheless, Colin Casey suddenly appeared out of nowhere, his eye sockets shooting machetes, his mouth clenching vile saliva, and his hair reaching to the heavens.

"Will you stop that agonizingly horrendous racket, at once!" he screamed as though his limbs were being amputated.

Nat and I protested with pained disbelief that anyone could judge such sweet melodies to be 'horrendous', but Colin had already summoned the YPBA security. Our blue friends had always been good to us, listening to our drunken rants, checking on us when we felt like death, and even risking their jobs on a daily basis by retrieving sandwiches for us out of the bin that the YPBA café hadn't sold that day. The last thing we wanted to do was give *them* a problem, so we just gave in and retreated with our spines curved like bananas, and our bodies riddled with enraged indignance. Admittedly the time was one o'clock in the morning, but that's not *that* late. We weren't near enough to any bedrooms to be disturbing anyone who was trying to sleep. We were in a noxious stupor at the time, so the racket we were making could possibly have been louder than we thought, but it still couldn't have been any real cause for complaint, surely! Colin Casey really was like an ever-returning bluebottle who's always buzzing into your mouth.

Another time, one of the YPBA lifts had jolted to a halt between floors. Myself, Colin and a few vacant-faced Leebock and Krappa donned residents had been stuck in there for a short but seemingly endless time, when Colin had the audacity to accuse me of interfering with the lift mechanism.

"If you don't immediately make this lift move again, I'll arrange for the police helicopter to hover outside your room every hour for the next two months!" he peevishly squealed

in my face, while I stayed motionless like a rock.

No words could have escaped my mouth at that point unless I had spat them like venomous bullets. No way could I have said anything back without saying something peevish, so I just didn't say anything, although I had plenty of things I wanted to say, and my quiet rage was bursting at the seams. I was relieved that the lifts galloped into movement again, although this could have made it look like I was giving in to his threats, and fixing the lift through the power of telekinesis or something.

Strangely, no-one else in the lift had even flickered an eyeball at the scene that had just occurred, not even one frown or snigger. This made me wonder where in the universe their spirit had got to. I had grave suspicions by then that the higher power that Old Col referred to as 'God', was really some other, ill-natured Being. I was filled with a lonely terror that I was the only person who could see that there was something not quite right about Colin.

More months went by, and all the usual things happened. I got rat-assed many times, and ran around at large in the community causing havoc. I became comatose and felt like I would die when I came round. I formed friendships, lost friendships, and got into all sorts of scrapes. I chain-smoked joints, enjoyed a few car chases, but became more and more like a dry frozen toad by day. One day, my Community Psychiatric Nurse came with news that I was being offered a permanent tenancy in some new flats nearby. This was just the new beginning I had been hoping for, and I accepted without hesitation.

But nothing could take my mind off Mr Casey. Every time I saw him I was left shitting venom in my boots. By now, I had experienced many infuriating and frightening incidents involving him, but one such incident left me irreversibly seething with toxic nuclear waste. This was when I witnessed Old Colin kicking a cat. Not just any old cat—the YPBA cat, Moonlight! And not just any old kick. I had slinked into the kitchen to see if there was any food left over from the YPBA bigwigs' meeting that day. Through the window I noticed Moonlight, stretching his legs outside the back of the YPBA kitchen, minding his own cat fur. A nanosecond later I viewed Colin galloping from nowhere towards Moonlight, decelerating slightly, and then shifting in that unmistakably twisted way that footballers do when they're taking a long shot. I immediately heard that nerve-piercing screeching yowling sound that cats make when they're fighting, and witnessed a black ball of fur, legs sprawling out, flying through the air! I was too terrified to hang around to see if Moonlight was OK, especially as Colin was now roaring with putrefied laughter. So I speedily scarpered. I spotted Moonlight again later, and he seemed OK, but that's not the point. From then on I wore a deep hatred for Mr Casey, which left my heart drumming with rage every time I saw him, or even just heard his voice. I was so infuriated by now, that my fury was beginning to overtake my fear.

Enjoying an intense but still-water anger, I played the long game and began to study Old Col. I had a month before I could move into my new flat. Surely I could do something about his antics before I left!

On first glance, Mr Casey didn't seem anything out of the ordinary. On the other hand, in a certain light, a discerning hyper-aware gaze such as my own could see that his eyes were actually quite inhuman. Depending on which way the sun was coming from, they were either lacy steel razors, or snake's eyes. No soul shone from behind them. Col's gaze somehow always appeared to be looking in on itself in a self-satisfied manner. It was plain to see that he was dangerous and devious, though this may have been unnoticeable to the untrained eye.

I could never get over my amazement that Colin Casey always seemed to mingle jovially with most folk around him, when he left such a great distaste in my mouth. Having witnessed his usual sneering sarcastic pleasantries, as well as some of his more blatant evil doings, more often than I had wished for, I now focused wholeheartedly on getting the better of him twice and for all. I needed to somehow lull him into a false sense of security so I could trick him into looking straight into my eyes. I might then be able to see the exact nature of the evil that lay behind his. For this dubious but necessary purpose, my ability to stare unnervingly could now be put to good use. Since being warned against staring at people by the psychiatrists, I had perfected a vacant stare, so convincing that even the devil himself wouldn't be able to tell that I might really be looking at him. Before long I got the chance to saunter over to the YPBA canteen for a chat with Mr Casey, and put this pièce de résistance to good use. I had received a message from Colin saying that I wasn't allowed to walk around the building in bare feet any-more. I had to have an explanation for this new rule. No way would I follow it unless there was a good enough reason to. I had enough trouble trying to stay grounded, without having to permanently place the sole of a shoe between myself and the floor! I entered the room in bare feet, looked directly at Colin's snake eyes with my blank stare, and purred,

"I trust you are in good health this evening Mr Casey? Ever so sorry to bother you but what, pray tell, is the rationale behind this new rule you have been so kind as to draw my attention to?"

Colin replied in a similar vein, although with a voice you would expect a lizard to talk with: "I'm ever so sorry Ms Eastwood, but the YPBA Health and Safety Regulations simply won't allow it."

"Is that so? Then I would be grateful if you could provide me with a copy of those regulations," I responded.

I detected a hint of exasperation in Colin's voice at this point: "Wer wer, I'm afraid that won't be possible."

"Oh, why ever is that?" I asked innocently.

In a lightning bolt, I realised that, while grasping for excuses, Colin happened to be, at that very moment, staring head on into my blank stare. It was then that I stung him good and proper, catching his eyes straight on. I was almost blinded by the garish red and yellow circles around the hollow black pupils. To not show any distress at that moment was one of the hardest things I've ever had to do in my life, but I managed it. "Hello Satan," I telepathized, with a knowing look on my face. Mr Casey, or whoever he really was, looked away in a scurry.

The old fellow's soul had been tampered with at the very least! His eyes might look normal to most people, but I had now endured the dubious pleasure of looking full on into them whilst they were looking into mine. I now knew for sure that it was really Beelzebub that Colin Casey must be referring to when he spoke about 'God'!

One hot, sunny occasion, not too many days later, as I emerged from a bender, I was startled to discover that Mr Casey was somehow in league with Peaky Dee, the YPBA drug-dealer. This untouchable resident fixture had lived at the far end of the top floor for longer than anyone could remember. Everyone knew he was a dealer and yet he never got busted. I had often scored malium from him when my brain had been brimming with a harsh and confused overload, but there was no time to meditate, and I was too ill to drink. On the day in question, out of the side of my eye, whilst waiting for the lift, I noticed Mr Casey shaking hands with Peaky, outside in the car park, thinking that no-one was looking. I'm not usually into eavesdropping, but I just had to hear what they were mumbling. Little did either of them know, I was that blackbird pulling at worms in a nearby flower-bed, when they had the following exchange:

"Now listen, and listen good," Mr Casey snapped. "You need to get a load more hero on hand, and it needs to be much more free-flowing. I've got a van load of newbies arriving any time now, and their welcoming party will be oohh such an easy opportunity."

"Nah worry blud", replied Peaky, in his deep dulcet tones.

Heartful, and forever aiming toward virtue, Peaky usually only dealt in much less harmful drugs. He was selfish though, and so ready to do whatever it took to keep his position and livelihood.

"Ah'll gladly bang it airt solidly until you say otherwoise," he re-assured Colin.

"Glad to hear it," exclaimed Colin Casey in his lizard-like tones, "Glad to hear it!"

I was horrified to hear what I was hearing. It dawned on me that Colin Casey must be involved in hijacking people's souls! The effects of this drug hero, otherwise known as 'orange', would loosen up these kids' souls just nicely for the purposes of the old Bristian fellow. And of course, the authorities turned a blind eye to the distribution of this particular drug, even encouraged it, knowing it kept troublemakers quiet, and other undesirables off the street, as long as they could get hold of it without too much trouble. Peaky represented his wares well by being a fitness freak, and sporting shiny golden shoulder muscles bulging from a white vest. He himself of course didn't use most of the drugs he was selling, but how were his customers to know that? They just saw how fit he looked and so believed that nothing they bought from him could be that harmful. And of course, the poor unsuspecting drug-users who used hero didn't realise that this particular drug was increasing the chance of their souls being lost. If they did realise this at some point down the line, by then they were past the point of caring.

Just at that moment, the reassuring hum of a minibus engine eased into the YPBA car park. Through the windows I could see wide-eyed teenagers, looking around with great expectations, and no idea of the possible danger they were about to be at risk of. My stomach was a barrelful of magnets. My blood thawing yogurt, my mouth drying almost to choking point. Colin Casey was looking for new recruits; young soldiers to join him in a never-ending Hell on earth. He had to be stopped!

I sidled over to greet the unsuspecting teenagers as they emerged. As expected, they displayed a variety of mugs, but were uniformly clad in labels, hoods, and caps. I welcomed them to the YPBA and they laughed and joked a bit with me. They were live wires, but they were flagging and ravenous, so I pointed them toward the kitchen where I knew a partially rancid buffet tea would be waiting for them.

I loitered near the pool table in the communal lounge, desperately hoping I could somehow prevent them from falling into Colin's horrifying trap. But soon I heard a weird siren, after which one of the girls I'd met earlier appeared from the kitchen, now devoid of any sparkle, and accompanied by a vague smell of decaying flesh. I was devastated to see that she already looked like a hero addict. It was too late. She would now be cast into a life of getting hero and more hero, which in turn would soon require her to become involved in dealing the stuff herself in order to pay for her own ration, and so that even more kids could be sent to Hell to keep the devil company. I asked her if the tea had been nice, but she wasn't now interested in socializing, and sloped off with her empty eyes and curved downwards face. I wondered where the others had got to and my nightmares were soon answered when, one by one, they all reappeared in the same way. I felt like a greenfly swimming against a tidal wave, as my shock gave way to horror. I was incapable of doing anything but record the sound of the siren.

Later that night on the phone, my bones shuddered as I learned from my theological historian friend Idris that the sound-wave of the siren that accompanied these kids' entrances from behind that fateful kitchen door was at exactly the right pitch for transporting human souls to Hell, but yet leaving their breathing bodies on earth. All I could manage to do that night was go down the Crown on Bornchurch Road and get absolutely hammered.

That night, in a telepathic dream, I learned that the soul of Mr Casey himself had some time ago become split in half; one half now being in Hell, the other half still on Earth simultaneously. This effect had occurred whilst Colin had performed a ritual under the effects of a manmade hallucinogen. The ritual in question had involved him playing a church organ whilst staring into a mirror lit with candlelight, and at the same time reciting the Lord's Prayer backwards. Since then, Colin had been no more than a useful hand tool for the devil's work on Earth. No-one will ever know if he had known at the time what the results of such an antic would be.

The next afternoon, I dragged myself downstairs, like a dying nauseous slug with a pierced and shattered head, only to observe Mr Casey quick march some of the new, now soulless looking kids into the music room, carrying ominous candles. Old Col was paying particular attention to an older boy called Fadam, who was exhibiting a blank but focused look on his face. I remembered him from yesterday. I had noticed that he seemed to be the most sensible one of the bunch. It was then that the alarming, chilling fact dawned on me: Colin Casey must be aiming to get a left-hand man to join him in his mission, and this boy's initiation day must be today! Fadam must be the one who, under Colin's instruction, was going to see to it that the new kids all became devoted new recruits! Certainly not wanting to miss anything, I shape-shifted into an ant and crawled under the door into the middle of the music room unnoticed, only to hear Colin instructing Fadam to learn to say the Lord's Prayer backwards, and even reverse all the words themselves. This would make the prayer almost unrecognizable! A momentary look of horror chased across Fadam's face. As if to reassure him, Mr Casey told him that it was just a chant often used by Buddhists who didn't take the Lord's Prayer seriously, and that it was good to be open to the ideas of other religions! Fadam screwed up his forehead and danced from one foot to the other as though his bowels were a volcano about to erupt. To try and calm him, old Col promised with intense earnestness to teach him the distorted version of the prayer on Sunday night after choir practice. He would play the old church organ to accompany him. This really was it! As a matter of emergency, Colin Casey had to be prevented from continuing his mission before it was too late!

It was no good reporting old Col to the Bristian Church, or to any other organisation for that matter. And there was no chance that I could bring myself to ask anyone else for help. During childhood, my family had insisted that my everyday practical skills were nonexistent, and I was still trying to prove to anyone who might notice, that this wasn't the case. As far as everyone else was concerned, Colin Casey was a very well respected member of the community anyway. At worst, most people just found him mildly annoying due to his cheese-grating voice. If I blurted out anything to anyone about the situation, they would probably accuse me of imagining things, just like my Mother and the mental health services often have.

It was now of utmost importance that Colin Casey was swiftly stopped in his tracks. And what better way to do this than through a powerful herbal concoction!

Long ago, when the church of the poisoned mind had first taken possession of these lands, herbalism had been banned throughout the whole continent, and crap food had been brought in to make sure that people were filled with the least goodness possible. People had been so terrified upon seeing herbal practitioners being burnt at the stake by the likes of the Colin Caseys of the time, that they didn't even talk about herbs any more. In the end, any herbal knowledge had been all but lost. But my great great great grandmother and grandfather had escaped by living deep in a wood with the wild boars of mid France. They had brought up their family there until a time when it had been safe enough to return to the community, though still keeping their practice underground. They had passed their knowledge on, down through the generations. My mother had taught me what I know. Even in the year 2021 however, it remains necessary to practice herbalism under a certain veil of secrecy as there is still a taboo attached to possessing such knowledge, unless of course you are a subsidiary of a company like Prickster & Gumble for example.

But, going back to Colin Casey, I knew full well from my previous dealings with demonic folk in rural Blemshire, that the best way to torture them into absolute submission was to con them into consuming something that was good for them. First, I sprinkled some magical herbal powder in Colin's hand gel, which he kept in the piano stool, and which I guessed he must use for keeping his fingers good for evil work. Over the coming days his hands became so agonizingly itchy that he scratched them down to the flesh. They were so painful that he was forced to have a break from playing his satanical organ music. He soon got wise to what the problem was, though he still didn't know that his hand gel had been tampered with; he just thought that he must have got sensitized to it, and so had simply refrained from using it.

And then the day arrived when I could move into my new flat. This fine cloudless day, I concocted a herbal tea for Colin, with some dried herbs that I had been saving for just such an occasion. The marvellous secret recipe included nettle, sage, dandelion, horsetail, thyme, honey and lemon; and in Mr Casey's cup I also included a little something that I couldn't quite remember the ingredients or provenance of, and hadn't really been sure what it had been in the first place.

Even the most poisoned and evil person would surely start becoming cleared of impurities and instilled with goodness upon drinking the potion I had meshed. But Mr Casey *needed* the impurities; they were necessary to lock one half of his soul onto Earth, so that his eyes could be a window for the devil to look through!

On that searing scorcher of a Bromford day, I arranged to meet Colin in the music room to talk about the possibility of coming back for piano lessons after I'd left the YPBA. I played a funeral march on the old church organ as he entered the room. I turned around and, with the most evil voice I could muster, asked him if he would like a cup of herbal tea. I gazed into his eyes with that same blank stare through which I had first sussed him out. Due to my brilliant acting he believed that I was as evil, if not more so, than he was, so he didn't think for one minute that the drink I gave him would be made from ingredients that were actually beneficial. He retched in disgust upon smelling it and I bantered with him telepathically that he'd gone soft. I reassured him that I had mixed the urine of rabid animals in it, along with the tears of someone who had just found out they had one of the deadly viruses that were being spread around the local hospitals. Well, what do you know, Mr Casey fell for it. Here he was like a kitten about to be butchered, with my heavenly herbal tea in his paws. I told him that the Devil had sent me to check that he still had what it took, seeing as he had not been sending many souls to Hell lately, being unable to play his organ music due to his fingers being out of action. I was grateful that Colin didn't summon up the Devil at that point to try and confirm whether this was true, as he believed me, and didn't want him to find out that he had hesitated.

"This will be just the ticket," he barked, and began to throw his herbal tea down in a long series of thirsty gulps, so as to prove to me that he was still on the degenerate side.

As the wonderful concoction hit his stomach, Mr Casey's skin began to hiss and steam: he was melting! He screamed an indescribable harmonic of shrillness that even the most powerful of evil beings would have been frightened of. This terrifying emanating consciousness actually *was* the devil, who had raced into Colin's body to see what was going on. Any piece of the person that Colin Casey had once been was now exiting his crumpling cadaver, his charred and sick half-soul groaning in agony. Evilness threw hot molten daggers from his eyes as his body shrank. An important disciple was being lost on Earth! Satanic organ music seemed to ring in the voice roaring,

"You will never get away with this!"

Smiling, I mused to myself that, this time, the sound of the organ music signaled Mr Casey's, and indeed Satan's own death knell.

"I'll get back in through someone else!" Mr Casey's body screamed like a giant roaring mosquito.

I must admit, I was terrified by the unfolding chain of events, but my poker face didn't show it. I was like a terrapin who'd just won a fight with a jealous crocodile. I was relishing my new found power to the point where my joy overcame my fright.

"Oh well," I replied, with just enough niceness to infuriate who-ever this being was before he descended back to Hell, "A woman's work will never be done."

Colin Casey's smoldering body was now slumped still on the floor. My heart was bouncing so forcefully that the thud was pounding in my ears. I knew that the only way the Devil could get me now was through fear, and any fear that I had ever had was now evaporating. I knew a fresh and welcome sense of wellbeing. I was as happy as a wasp on a toffee apple in the knowledge that I had exterminated Colin Casey, but I couldn't just relax. There was no time for celebration; not right now anyway. I needed to get rid of any evidence that might incriminate me.

There was a cozy kitchen just off the music room. I washed the cup that Mr Casey's tea had been in, taking as much time as I dared. I tried to make sure that every trace of whatever the un-known substance in the herbal tea had been, disappeared safely down the plughole, just in case it was somehow known or dis-covered that it was me who had given Colin the tea. To ensure it wouldn't look like someone had tried to destroy the evidence, I put the cup to Colin's mouth. As though inserting a scorpion's gum shield, I wiped a bit of his saliva at the edges of it. More and more breathless with anguish, I then slopped in a bit of tea that didn't have the unknown substance in it, so it looked like that was all I had given him. Last, I pressed Mr Casey's finger ends on the cup in places where they would have held it. As for any evidence that the unknown substance had ever been in my pos-session, I was just going to have to hope for the best on that one. I had the scrunched up Rizla in my pocket that it had been kept in. I didn't hesitate to make a roll-up with it, and lit it, whilst bracing myself for a quick exit.

Of course, I had done nothing wrong, but I didn't wish to be discovered at the scene of Colin Casey's final demise, when this could be misconstrued as being a murder scene. So I began to flee, with all the jerky speed my shaky disintegrating body could muster. There were a group of serious-faced people staring at me in the lobby as I ran past. This was disappointing. I would have preferred the encouragement of a cheer at least. I didn't get very far. The police must have already been called as there were white vehicles with bright yellow and blue markings, and blinking glares outside. Mr Casey, the devil, and I must have been making more of a din than I had realised. Either that or someone had spied Mr Casey's death scene through a crack in the door. As I exited the main entrance of the YPBA, a group of navy uniforms were coming at me, on the attack. I tried to karate them off as best I could, throwing my cigarette to the car thieves, who were now kindly cheering, until I was pinned face down on my car, handcuffed with my hands behind my back. I was shoved and bundled away to the local police station to be strip-searched and questioned.

Whether sane, insane, or just plain autistic, I was under suspicion of having killed a man who was perceived to be an upstanding member of the community. But I was certain they wouldn't be able to make any charges stick. Herbalists might still be seen as witches by some people, but surely there's no law against giving someone herbs that are usually wholly *good* for human beings. There might indeed be evidence within Colin's corpse of the presence of the unknown substance, but Colin could have taken that at any time for all they knew. As far as I could think, there shouldn't be any real evidence that that stuff had ever been in *my* possession. I decided not to admit, even to the duty Solicitor, that there had been anything in the concoction other than the ingredients that are known to be good for people. "How was I to know that Colin would have such a violent allergic reaction to such harmless herbs?" I would plead in my defence.

I may have broken the law. I may have killed someone. I may have done this accidentally or on purpose, but at least I had saved the lives of some YPBA residents by doing so. I didn't feel at all bad that it may have been me who had instigated old Col's demise. I cared about people and that's why I had to annihilate him. I had once asked a Buddhist meditation teacher if it was ok to kill people who I observed to be killing other people. I can't quite remember what the answer was, but I had interpreted it to mean that it *was* ok. Mr Casey hadn't been killing people, but he might as well have been, as the bodies of those poor teenagers hadn't contained the same souls after his meddling. It just wouldn't be fair if I became incarcerated because of Colin Casey's death. And it wouldn't be at all fair if they locked me back up in the psychiatric hospital.

Down at the grey box of a police station I met with the nondescript duty Solicitor Victor Bartholomew. I told him about the herbal tea and how I'd been trying to make friends with Mr Casey, as I had wanted him to teach me how to play the piano. I was very upset about his demise!

Victor informed me that they'd decided I'd planned it in icy blood because I was anti-Bristian, but not to worry as he'd do his best to try and get them to understand my side of things. Otherwise, it would be up to the court to decide whether I should go to prison or a secure psychiatric hospital. With the paradoxical ambiguity of autism bearing down on the situation like an elephant in a china shop, who knows what the court's decision would be. My ticker was punching the inside of my head like a boxer's fist, as if to make sure I kept my wits about me. The prison option would have a clear-cut time scale, but less opportunity for tranquilizers and molly-coddling. If I wanted this then I needed to show I understood the situation I was in, admit what I'd done and explain my motives as the rational though ill motives of a bad person. The hospital option would have no known end date, and would be risking brain damage through prolonged exposure to harmful medications. If I wanted this option, I could easily get it by shrieking with laughter at everything they said, or singing nursery rhymes in response to their questions, and acting generally like I didn't know what they were going on about. My mind raced, but I struggled to reach a conclusion. What the hell should I do?

I decided just to tell them the whole truth (apart from the bit about the unknown substance), and hope for the best. They probably wouldn't believe me, but at least I'd be staying true to myself, even if I was risking an indefinite stay in a hospital. Once in hospital, I might even be able to convince the professionals to let me out, even earlier than prison would allow for. And if I remained on my best behavior, surely they wouldn't inject me with anything *too* harmful.

Victor seemed to think that I had a good case and drably reassured me that there was no need to fret. He wrote everything down, and then disappeared for an eternity. A loud hollow banging echo of doors signaled his return with a couple of plainclothes police officers and two attentive psychiatrists who were to observe my interrogation. The interview tape was rolling but I was too preoccupied to listen to anything that was being said, my pulse thumping in my ears, my mind going back over things, trying to make sure there were no flaws in my story, but never quite getting through to the end of it. They were asking me questions and trying to get me to talk, but I couldn't think straight, let alone get any words out. I could hear distant murmuring about 'imagining things', 'refusing to cooperate', 'autism', 'influence of alcohol' and 'obstructing justice.' Good old Victor passed his notes to me so I could read from them. But, hang on a minute; Victor's notes just looked like some sort of weird gobbledygook. They didn't make any sense whatsoever:

"menA, reve dna reve rof, yrolg eth dna rewop eht, modgnik eht si eniht roF, live morf su reviled tuB, noitatpmet otni ton su daeL, su tsniaga ssapsert ohw esoht evigrof ew sA, sessapsert ruo su evigrof dnA, daerb yliad ruo yad siht su evig, nevaeh ni si ti sa htrae nO, enod eb lliw yht, emoc modgnik yht, eman yht eb dewollah, nevaeh ni tra ohw rehtaF ruO."

My blood ran cold as I realized what I was deciphering. I was frantic to stay calm, and tried to bring to mind that terror was my biggest foe here. But Victor shoved me half off the chair, pushing his notes towards me. He looked up. As my eyes met his, lightning bolted through my body as I saw red and yellow snake eyes. I scanned the room in a panic and was blinded by sharp gleams of red and yellow from every single eye in the room. All mouths were wide and turned up at the edges, showing sharp rotten gappy teeth. Victor's face a wrathful evil grin, his voice a grinding metallic scream, demanded:

"Now read this to us!!"

I involuntarily released a murderous primal scream, though no sound came out. All my nerves were writhing on fire one second, and then the next moment I was a rushing chainsaw of adrenalin. I became a savage octopus tiger, extremities flying everywhere like helicopter blades, teeth biting, in a desperate attempt to do them as much damage as possible, before they overpowered me once again. Finally, I felt a gentle breeze on my haunches and the familiar bee sting on my buttock. I surrendered into shock, bliss, and luxury, where nothing matters any more. I glimpsed blood on some of their faces, even managed a smirk, lolling with ease and comfort as they carted me away sideways.

weighting/the machine:
whut mad[ness] is mad[e] uv

PHIL SMITH

```
i am      waiting        to die.
i am      weighting      to die.
i am      writhing       to die.
i have been
     waiting and
     weighting and
     writhing and
     way-thing          to die all my life.
across the boundaries
inside and outside
of this lifetime
i tried to hurry it.
i tried to move
it along faster
than it wanted to go
with pills and hills
```

and chills and drills.
no luck, at least not
yet—or, perhaps, the luck
is that i haven't managed
to hurry it along.
that others haven't
been able to hurry it
along for me at times
and ways that i didn't
want or choose.

•

"It is sometimes an appropriate response to reality to go insane."
—Philip K. Dick

•

on this day
i sit on a pile
of firewood that i've stacked
above the brook
looking up at the autumn
sky, watching ravens[1]
croak and swoop and
flip upside down for

---

1   the mad hatter asked alice, "why is a raven like a writing-desk?" when al-
     ice said she didn't know, and asked in response why, he said, "i haven't the
     slightest idea." hatters were mad from the mercury, you know, which made
     better felt than the piss that they used to use.

a moment in wind
growing colder by the minute.
the pile of wood is held together
by the weight of the chunks
that make it up
and gravity that pulls it
down, holds it
tight, and at the same
time tries to pull it
apart. my thoughts and
feelings are held
together and pulled
apart in the same
way, the gravity^2 of my
life pulling and pushing
sometimes pulled and
pushed by me
sometimes pulled and
pushed by others.

•

"...I have found both freedom and safety in my madness; the freedom of loneliness and the safety from being understood..."
—Kahlil Gibran

•

---

2   gravity is the way stuff is pulled and pushed together, sometimes stuff that
    belongs, sometimes stuff that doesn't.

the Machine is
always working.
it never gives up.
the smallest of flywheels
tiny pistons, teensy
valves, driving the engine
of capitalism forward
thrusting the arrow
of buy more, sell
more through our soulhearts
destroying our bodyminds
with chemicals and poisons
and the things that make
us twist in the wind
always twisting, writhing.
until we die hanging
by a rope from a
tree
branch.

•

"In a mad world, only the mad are sane."
—Akira Kurosawa

•

we were driving.
we'd been driving all
the late summer morning

and longer
(it was coming to mid-afternoon now)
and we stopped for gas.
she went in for a snack.
coming back to the car
she became angry
incensed, enraged
for the life of me i
couldn't figure out why.
she got behind the wheel
peeled out of the gas station
shot toward the on-ramp
like something out of a cannon
headed to the highway.
she continued driving
faster and faster
aiming directly toward a concrete
overpass that i was certain
she intended to drive straight
into in order to kill us both
as i'd heard that others did
from time to time.
i'm quite sure that's what she
planned to do. i was
literally afraid for my
life, and hers as well.[3] terrified
i climbed into the back seat.
she didn't hit the overpass.

---

3   it happened in an instant and it took a very long time (my whole life).

she slowly grew more calm.
i ended it two days later. this
actually happened. also things
that actually happened are
all the times that i saw and see
cars of the same color and
sometimes shape and i completely
freak[4] right the fuck out. two years
after it all went down i finally
realized that these were connected.
i'm slow like that.

·

"Too much sanity may be madness—and maddest of all: to see life
as it is, and not as it should be!"
—Dale Wasserman

·

the Machine is out
to do one thing only:
to keep us all in
line. it has a host
of tools at its
disposal to make this
happen:
police.

---

4   the body remembers what was done to the heart.

physicians.
judges.
forensic investigators.
nurses.
psychologists.
teachers.
administrators.
the psy scion tists.
these are deployed throughout
every industry to insure
that all follow steadfastly
in line behind those ahead
and leading those who snake
along in back. deviation in
thought and action is
not permitted. these tools
employ a variety of technologies
developed for their needs:
drugs.
therapeutic protocols.
72-hour holds.
seclusion.
mechanical and physical restraint.
incarceration.
the psy calm plex.

•

"It is no measure of health to be well adjusted to a profoundly
 sick society."
—Jiddu Krishnamurti

•

you know about ACEs,
right? adverse childhood
experiences? answer a
series of questions
about your childhood, count
up the number of experiences.
people who have a score of 4
or higher are at significantly
increased risk for
   "alcoholism,
    drug abuse,
    depression,
    and suicide attempt...
    poor self-rated health...
    sexually transmitted disease...
    The seven categories
    of adverse childhood experiences
    were strongly interrelated
    and persons with multiple categories
    of childhood exposure
    were likely to have multiple
    health risk factors later in life[5]"

---

5   (Felitti, V., Anda, R., Nordenberg, D., Williamson, D., Spitz, A., Edwards, V.,
     Koss, M., & Marks, J., 1998, p. 245).

yeah. so.
my score? a 5.
i don't have all the stuff listed
above. i *am* Mad. was i Mad before
all the things
happened to me?
dunno. mebbe. prolly.

•

"Sometimes, to regain sanity, one had to acknowledge and embrace
 the madness."
—Morgan Rhodes

•

the Machine keeps us all
working for it, working
with it, working on it,
working. the Machine
does its best work in
darkness, hidden even
from those who built and
maintain it, who house
and ensure its safety. the
Machine does its best work
in complete secrecy, known
to only a very, very few.

•

"...the madness of the world tries to colonize you: from the outside
in, forcing you to live in its reality."
—Jeff VanderMeer

•

it's the end of april
and it's snowing again
or still. it didn't snow
yesterday. so the
fact that it's snowing
today is like welcoming
back an old friend
but one i'm not so
sure i really want to
see again. ever. in
a few days it will
be may, a month
that i have come
to hate. though
april is the cruelest
month, what comes
after is not much
good either. i
dislike it for the
anniversaries[6] it
carries. there are
worse—summer is

---

6   the body remembers what day it is and what happened on that day even
when the mind doesn't remember.

no fun at all—but
may brings up things
that i'd rather not
think about. day
in, day out. same
shit. so i get through
this may, and then
start on getting ready
for another. perhaps
i'll get to it. perhaps
i won't. there's
only one way to find out.
in the meantime it's
the end of april and
it's snowing. again.
or still.

•

"How can we live in a mad world without going mad ourselves?"
—Matt Haig

•

the Machine creates
a language and a thinking
and a being in which
certain very specific people
are demonstrably and
monstrously and certifiably

and completely and
provably outside
the boundaries of
what is considered
to be rational
thought. the Machine does
this by creating people
and words and rational
theories that sort those
who are by definition
irrational, and so incapable
of making decisions for
themselves and others
from those who are
by definition rational
who are capable of
making decisions for
themselves and others
including specifically those
who are by definition
irritatingly and irrepressibly
irrational.

•

[there is] "...a correlation between rising rates of mental distress
and the neoliberal mode of capitalism..."
—Mark Fisher

•

the length of this year
is something that is
almost impossible[7]
to measure. it is not
made of days or
weeks or hours or
months or minutes. it
is made of the number
of times i saw another
human person[8] (this
occurred about once a
week). it is measured by
the number of times I
intentionally and deliberately
touched another human
person (this has not happened
in a year). it is made of
the number of times i lay
on the floor crying aloud
(too numerous to count
too many to think of).

.

"Life without madness is mediocrity."
—Nelou Keramati

---

7   time is something we made up; it's not real. it's something the Machine uses
to keep us all in line.

8   i saw many persons but they weren't human. they were tree persons and fawn
persons and hummingbird persons and water water water persons.

•

the Machine does
its job day after month
after year after decade
after generation, powered
by those of us who climb
on to its treadmill to turn
all its workings, directed
by the wypipo who never
worry about their next
meal or where to send
their children to school
or if they'll be able to afford
their next car or when they
might be able to go on vacation
or… they sit at their little desks
and push their little buttons and
drink their little expensive coffees
from the shop across the street
that they don't even need to get
up from their desk to go to, they
just send "the girl" because that's
her job, am i right? it all hums
along just the way it's supposed
to, and if some people get chewed
up in the process, it's their own
fault anyway, they don't want to
get ahead anyway, if they did they'd

do something about it do something
about it dosomethingaboutit.

•

she came to me in
the morning. "last
night," she said, "while
you were asleep, I went
through your things."
she looked at me.
i thought, *what the actual
fuck?*, but didn't say it
out loud. "oh?" i said.
"yes," she said. "i knew
it wasn't the right thing to
do, but i had to. i was called
to do it." i thought, *called
to do it? what does that
even mean?* but didn't say
it out loud. "oh?" i said.
"yes," she said. "i went through
your things while you were
sleeping, which i knew was the
wrong thing to do, but i had to do it.
and had to tell you that i did,
otherwise i wouldn't be able to live
with myself." she looked at me.
i thought, *ok. let me get this straight.*

you went through my things, which
you knew to be the wrong thing
to do, but you couldn't live with
yourself if you didn't tell me you
did the wrong thing, as if that
justifies somehow doing the wrong
thing, but didn't say it out loud.
"oh," i said. "yes," she said.
i thought, *this is kinda*
fucking weird, but didn't
say it out loud. "yes," she
said, and looked at me.
"oh?" I said. "yes," she
said. she looked at me.
what the fuck? i
thought, but didn't say
out loud. i thought,
am i missing something here?
but didn't say it out loud.
"it proves it, you know," she
said, looking at me. i thought, *i*
am definitely missing something
here, but didn't say it out loud.
"what's that?" i said. "you know
what i mean," she said. *no,*
actually, i don't, I thought, but
didn't say it out loud. "what does
it prove?" i said. she looked at
me. i just stared at her.
it seems to me that it proves

that you think it's ok for you
to go through my things without
asking me, i thought, but
didn't say out loud.
months later, she wrote to me
that she was someone who
could always be trusted.
uh, no, I thought, and
said it out loud. i guess
i can add trust issues to
the list
of things that i have.

•

"We want a few mad people now. See where the sane ones have landed us!"
—George Bernard Shaw

•

the Machine is very efficient.
the Machine is very effective.
the Machine is very fast.
the Machine was built from the ground up by wypipo.
the Machine knows what it is doing.
the Machine grinds ndn's into the dirt.
the Machine doesn't question it's work.
the Machine is racist and doesn't know it.
the Machine makes more of itself.

the Machine actively hurts queer people.

the Machine constantly refines what it does.

the Machine relies on political power.

the Machine uses hegemonic masculinity to its advantage.

the Machine locks up people who try to shut it down and puts them behind bars forever and ever and ever amen.

●

"'Crazy' is a word that does some dirty cultural work. It is a flip way of referencing mental illness, yes. But it's also a slippery label that has little to do with how a person's brain works and everything to do with how she is culturally received. Calling someone crazy is the ultimate silencing technique. It robs a person of her very subjectivity."
—Amanda Hess

●

three deer yearlings
run through the field.
are they the triplets i
saw last year? they
don't say. a short while
later, a bald eagle flies
north up the shore
screaming. it says too
much in a way i don't
understand. they're all
i have—when i had to

have surgery a couple
of weeks ago, i had to
call the local senior center to
get someone to drive
me to the hospital
and then back to
the cabin. but
really, i don't want other
humans near me right
now—mostly what they
do is cause more pain, more
trauma, and of those i
have enough right now
thank you very much.

•

"The idea that anyone is mentally well all of the time is a delusion…"
—Merri Lisa Johnson

•

what is so disturbing
and most distressing
about the Machine
is that it is created out
of whole cloth by people.
actual real people
with human bodies
and real addresses.

the Machine benefits
those human people
and disadvantages
a great many more
(some human
some not).
that the Machine
could be dismantled
is real news
that many deny.

•

"At the edge of madness you howl diamonds and pearls."
—Aberjhani

•

and so here is the end of it. I am filled to overflowing with madness, which at times brings me great pain, immense sorrow, extraordinary fear. i also know that without it i could not experience the tremendous joy, outlandish passion, extreme curiosity, and boundless connection to all that surrounds me. it is part of me, part of my essential nature. i would no more give it up than i would give up the left side of my face. it's who i am.
take me as i am, or do not take me at all.

RIDICULOUS ROLLINGONTHEFLOOREFERENCES

Felitti, V., Anda, R., Nordenberg, D., Williamson, D., Spitz, A., Edwards, V., Koss, M., & Marks, J. (1998). *Relationship of childhood abuse and household dysfunction to many of the leading causes of death in adults: The Adverse Childhood Experiences (ACE) Study. American Journal of Preventive Medicine 14(4), 245–258.*

cat-Pigeon and Bird-woman

JACQUIE PRUDER ST. ANTOINE

It began and I became...

oh, when was it? Hard to say, really. I am not able to give you a day, even a year seems too fluid. Suppose if I had to pinpoint it, I'd say it was when I knew. I don't know if other Mad people have their *knowing*, but it is clear when I came to *know* my Madness. It was always there.

Cold, hard, smooth

Cold, hard, smooth

Cold, hard—smoooooooooth

Somedaysomeoneelseisgonnaliveinthisapartmentandnever-knowIevenexisted

NO.

Coldhardsmooth, cold hard smooth

Youllbeinthegroundandturningtodustandthereisnobeyondthereis-justdarkdarkdarkand

theyllbeinyourhouseandneverknowyouwereapersonnnnnn

It is a stomach churn and a weird neck feeling. Weird neck feeling? Yeah, unfortunately those words are the best I have for the bodily moment of a thought spiral. The first time I knew I was made Mad (Can I trademark it? I'm gonna trademark it.) I was living in a square apartment with a short fridge, heavy furniture, and cold, cinder block walls. If you have ever lived in a furnished apartment, you know the furniture. It's heavy because they don't want you to take it. The edges are harsh. The fabric on the couch is a rough weave. Even if you cover it, you know it doesn't want you there.

I didn't become Mad in this little box made for one little human person (and in my case a fifteen pound cat I snuck in named Pigeon). I am convinced I was Made Mad™ but I came to know it in this tiny box-room. Bars on the windows and pipes that leaked in the bathroom under the sink.

Drip. Drip.

I came to know that drip drip dripppping because I spent so many days on the floor of the bathroom. Shove a pink towel underneath to catch the water and prevent rot.

But still, it dripped.

Drip, drip, drip.

Drip, drip, drip.

Cold, hard, smooth.

Cold, hard, smooth.

If you close your eyes and slow your racing heart, you might just be able to hear it now.

Careful...

    quiet...

        see?

           There it is.

You feel it in your chest.

Now quiet again and I will tell you a story. I get the feeling if you have made it here, you're one. A Mad one. Probably a pissed off one, too. So feel that race in your chest and churn in your stomach and know my story is as much your story. You have lots of stories and now my stories are yours to hold. After all, "one story always begets another" (Poole & Ward, 2013, p. 100). A story, now no longer mine but ours... Maybe if you're lucky two. These are stories "shrouded in secrecy—hidden or silenced stories that may shame others into acknowledging truths we haven't yet dared to tell" (Adams, 2017, p. 70-71).

9(teen)

Pigeon, who is not a pigeon but a cat, wanders the space between the dresser (which happens to be built into the wall... remember what I told you about the heavy furniture they think you'll steal) and bedroom door. "Hrrrrruuuu... Hrrrruuuu..... Pbrrrr-rraw, pbrrrr-rraw, aaaahhhhrrrww...."

Pigeon-cat has been my companion since she was a kitten, adopted from a life of drudgery on a farm in a small northern Michigan town with one stoplight where everyone knows everyone's secrets. Despite being a fifteen pound cat, Pigeon makes cooing sounds like that of a bird. I consider this to be one of our most special bonds—just two bird creatures living in human and cat bodies.

"He who calls the creatures by their true names
has power over them" (Griffin, 1978, p. 22)

    I claim no domination over this friend

    and call her by bird-name,

    wishing to wield no power,

    wishing never to create her world with my words.

In fact, I see no separation between human-woman-person and bird-cat-person. To differentiate and hyper-separate myself from this companion, to exert or justify dominance or conquest of this friend would be to subordinate (Plumwood, 2002) her as *mine*.

There is no radical separation, no "Other" deficient in relation to the center (Plumwood, 2002).

And it is said *"that animals do not think. That animals move automatically like machines... if animals could think, they might have immortal souls...*

And it is said that the souls of women are small"
(Griffin, 1978, p. 19-20).

She calls to me, her cooing womanly and questioning. She calls to me, a bird-cat,

knowing that a bird-woman will hear.

Certain someone is going to find out I have a cat where cats aren't allowed, hastily I build her a nest in a drawer. When I sleep I dream of her wandering the halls while I search frantically. The hallway carpet is dirty and old, even in my dreams. I pull open another drawer and drape a blanket over, creating a small, cave-like tent. Imagine being small enough to fit inside, curled in the guarded dark. Safe. The drumming of her throat signifies her appreciation as she tucks her body inside this quiet den. It soothes her, the tension and turmoil seeping out as her spine relaxes.

With quick breaths I return to the bed. It can never be *my* bed. The bed (like all the other furniture) belongs to this purgatory, a place between childhood and what life will look like in a future where I hope I can buy my own things. For now, I sleep on a borrowed bed, wash dishes in a borrowed sink, and sit in a shivering lump in a borrowed shower. I lay under *my* pink floral quilt (a gift from my mother, truly *mine*), my back against the cinder block wall. It is never dark in the city.

It is a thought that churns my empty stomach.

I begin my nightly panicked meditation,

Cold, hard, smooth.

Cold, hard, smooth.

coldhardsmoothcoldhardsmooth

COLDHARDSMOOTHCOLDHARDSMOOTHCOLD-

HARD—

Somedayyouwon'texistanymoreandwhenyoudietherisnothing.

No, no, no—don't think it. Don't think it.

you'llbedeaddeaddeadandit'llbedarkdarkdark

No, nonononononononononononononononononono.

No.

Don't think it.

Cold. Hard. Smooth. Cold. Hard. Smooth.

In this agitated study, hours pass. Some pass unnoticed, others crawl slowly. I haunt the three small rooms of this in-between place. Pacing the galley kitchen, I imagine my frenzied route leaves imprints on the cracked tile floor. Laying facedown on carpet in the adjoining living room/dining room/everything else room, I scratch my fingernails on the flat weave. Shower on as hot as I can bear, I crouch in a ball on the floor of the tub. I find myself in each place, unsure how I got there and how long I have been there. Pigeon watches faithfully from her den. In a spiral, time is endless and all at once. Waiting for morning to break, there are times I am sure I won't survive to see day. Can this hostile purgatory become my forever dwelling? I fixate on this idea, that these beleaguered hours are an afterlife where I am trapped and the time outside these walls is a projection.

Do other people think about their life being a dream?

A bright street light outside the barred window casts a flickering yellow haze of timelessness through the sturdy glass panes. The windows only open an inch or two. Midnight or noon, the light never changes. It is never dark here, another thought that races through my bones and veins as I lay in the eternal twitching gleam. Type 1 diabetics require more insulin and rates of cancer go up among teachers who work under these lights (Havas, 2008). Like a parakeet jailed in a pet store, I wither under this constant glow. Creatures, whether big or small, were never meant to be kept in boxes.

"This is the room I have never been in.

This is the room I could never breath in." (Plath, 1981, p. 218)

Tape black fabric to the walls, run a fingernail along the groove between the cinder blocks. Repeat incantations, *coldhardsmoothcoldhardsmoothcoldhardsmooth* to ward off the prickling conspiracies that race through my synapses. Count. Count some more, but only ever to six. I imagine the counting casts a protective spell around me. If I can make it to six, I can start over again. If I can make it to six, then I am still alive. If I can make it to six, I am closer to day.

When the small battery-operated alarm clock on the bedside table clangs, I know it is morning. How can something the size of my palm be my tether to now? It tugs the rope tied to my waist, pulling me back to materiality (a great service for which I am intensely grateful). The light remains the same in this haunted house and the hours have simultaneously dragged and slipped by with racing monologues, echoing loud-speaker repetitions, festering intrusions. A last jerk from the clock and I am back in the apartment that is the in-between and never can or will be mine. Back to the bed that isn't my bed and the room that isn't my room. Laundry still lays in a pile. The small table in the corner is still covered in papers. Dirty dishes still wait in the sink. Soup, from how many days ago I can't remember, stays covered.

Once I threw away a dish because I couldn't bear to wash it.

The idea of it was more than I could stomach. Looking at it just sitting in the sink, day after day after day. Even thinking about washing it was

so.

intensely.

exhausting.

I threw it away.

Soon I threw away more.

I ready myself for the outside, a fluffing of my feathers, smoothing of my fronds. Assemble the pieces that maintain an illusion. Curling iron. Lotion smeared across the jawline. Pink adorns chapped, chewed lips. Sensible shiny shoes with a thick strap. Fasten a button. Sweater. I recall a high school friend mocking me because I wore sweaters instead of hoodies... hoodies don't position you as a responsible-got-it-together-future-teacher-4.0-student-girl-lady. Sweaters in lush purple do. Purple sweaters keep you safe. Purple sweaters keep you free.

Construct myself, erecting a building instead of existing as a bird-woman, all in hopes of performing as a sane-bright-smiling-palatable-pretty-human-woman. Forge steel femurs and glass cheekbones, erasing the possibility of being a human-person "constructed as wrong/sick/disordered/anxious/depressed/in need of in-/outpatient care because of how they expressed and communicated the pain" (Poole & Ward, 2013, p. 103). When I am a bird-woman, I am delicately curved collarbones, papery patterned birch bark, a splattering of crimson on a tawny feather, lush and sweet-smelling soil, the heat of a dancing flame in a wood-burning fireplace. When I am a human-person, it requires tools, permits, labor, symmetrical lumber, screws and nails, graded timber, a general contractor.

> *"Trees growing in the forest should be*
> *useful trees"* (Griffin, 1978, p. 59).

There are rules a person can follow to pass as one of the normals, they are unwritten but most of you reading probably already know these rules. One of my rules is dress with flair. If I wear the emerald wool pea coat, people say "Wow, what a great coat!" and they don't think you need to be sent to a doctor, given medication, or evaluated. A great and noteworthy coat is a gateway to another world. It serves both as your personality and as a suit of armor. People who wear nice coats are squared away nicely as decent and typical, even enviable (because emerald is a universally flattering tone, I have found).

Stepping out into the December sun, I tuck the incursions away. Into the fuschia box adorned with magazine clippings my sister made for me the hauntings go. There they reside from 9 to 5. Only someone who has felt despair could take such gentleness and care in crafting such a box. For this box I am immensely grateful, so grateful I cry to think of it even now. Fifteen years later this box remains a treasure. A box like this is the secret to staying out of the rooms where they won't let you out—an imposed silence by "expert psychiatric discourse and chemical treatment" (Russo, 2016, p. 59). A neat box, preferably one crafted by another feeler.

With the lid returned to the box, I press on. Little pebbles of cat food pour into a ceramic bowl and Pigeon-cat cries out in appreciation, the sound a cooing that returns me to my body. Her yellow-gold eyes meet mine. I run fingers through her decadent downy softness. A cat-bird and a bird-woman in a borrowed room with borrowed furniture. I wonder if it'll always be like this.

Down the stairs. 123456. Onetwothreefourfivesix. 123fourfivesix. Down I spiral to the ground floor (my building has no elevator). Down I go and out into the winter sun, the cold air stealing my breath as the sun cascades over my whole body. It is a moment of luxury and carnal pleasure.

I imagine myself a starling, emerald iridescent feathers catching sunlight.

Although a starling is too generous,

even in the great coat.
Down the hill
and up the stairs.
Count them,

> *One23four56*
> *123-45six*
> *1too3fore5siiiix*

Up we go, up we go to the sixth floor,
to sit at a desk and

> *tick-tick on a typewriter*
> *(why are we using a typewriter in the early 2000's?)*
> *Each keystroke a harsh metallic staccato,*
>> *separatedandarticulate.*
> *As it is demanded*
>> *that forest trees grow straight and tall,*
>> *without knots,*
>> *to bear the best board, so too*
>>> *must a woman be a master typist,*
>>> *diplomatic and warm,*
>>> *stylish and tidy* (Griffin, 1978).

Back down the stairs (onetwothreefourfivesix, 123456), to a small counter where they sell foods for sleep-deprived and hung-over students. Their offerings consist of muffins and candy bars mostly. I trek here for a daily meal, out of habit more than hunger. You can subsist easily on an Odwalla bar (when and why did they stop making Odwalla bars?) and apple a day. Losing weight—another unwritten rule. Instant compliment, instant conversation starter.

This is the story of my sisters, but I don't know it. It is the story of my mother and her mother. An aunt. A friend. A mentor.

Typewriters, nibbled apple skins, handsome coats, dread in the night.

It is unspoken and guarded, the great secret of my womanhood. It is not an *I* story or a *me* story. It is a *We* story, but one we keep from our daughters and sons and children. Someday I will learn the secrets of this *"place where everyone is a daughter"* (Griffin, 1978, p. 171) and the wisdom that comes with growing crooked through cracks in the sidewalk. *"We grow thin. We are peevish. We are irritable. We have fits of crying. We cannot sleep at night... We exhibit madness. We are melancholy. We touch ourselves. We cannot help touching ourselves. We grow morbid. We believe we will be struck dead"* (Griffin, 1978, p. 91).

I believe I will be struck dead. I fearfully wait for it.

Reports filed, envelopes licked, Blue Book submitted.

I flee out into the cold, late afternoon sun. December wind burns as it dances across flesh, I open my ribcage and turn my face to the sun. There is beauty in it. Madness is a beauty I cannot spurn. I am utterly grateful for it. I drink in the stinging rays striking eyelids, burning bright light through thin derm into each hazel iris. The sadness makes this beauty possible. Wrapped in the arms of the sacred,

"Space in which there is no center" (Griffin, 1978, p. 172).

Though I stand in a concrete hub surrounded by unattractive square buildings, the sensual experience of it is profound. The appreciation and delight despair allows me is unspeakably holy.

The trilling call of my small feathered friend, chicka-dee-dee-dee rings through my ears. In her cheerful song I hear whispered sadness, unspoken otherness. My heart outpours gratefulness for her story. I doubt that anyone of sound mind has ever experienced this enchantment.

9teen&One-teen

We are urged to tell our stories to the logic-makers,

      the knowy-knowers, the sense-doers, the explainers and the prescribers and the diagnostic list checkers.

If you're reading this, then you are one of the ones who feels/is it in the bodymindsoul. I have already told you that these stories are not my stories but our stories. I'd bet you have thrown away dishes and worn green coats, too. So you won't be surprised to read that as years pass, the Mad doesn't go away. Even if you take the medicine or talk to the nice (or the not-so-nice) doctor or check in for a stay. It never goes away. And truth be told, I do not wish it away. I keep these parts and pieces and bits of broken glass safe from prying eyes so the list-carrying NO/knowy-knowers[1] cannot take it away. It can never go away because there is no *it*. The Madness is me and I am the Madness. To rid myself of it would be to erase myself of me.

---

1   Who and what is a "knower" and what is considered "knowledge" determines which voices are acknowledged. For Mad people, external experts (e.g. teachers, lawyers, doctors, psychiatrists, etc.) have traditionally been seen as knowers capable of making decisions for those considered mentally ill (Starkman, 2013; Russo & Beresford, 2015). Rather than seeing Mad people as knowers, social scientists have long taken the approach that these individuals are subjects who can be interpreted by experts (Russo & Beresford, 2015). Mad studies scholars reject this notion and place Mad perspectives at the center of knowledge formation. Similarly, those in EcoJustice education question the knowers and knowledge that are granted value in a Western culture. Scientific knowledge is described as "more certain, objective, unemotional, and culturally removed than other forms of knowledge" (Martusewicz, 2019, p. 123). Indigenous, local, and cultural knowledge (Martusewicz, Edmundson, & Lupinpacci, 2015; Martusewicz, 2019) is erased and/or discounted.

A night without stars.

Or,

       at the very least,

             a star without night.

And these knowers have science and a scientific method to prove their knowing. "Impartial, disengaged reason" (Plumwood, 2003, p. 20) is promoted as neutral and the ultimate in knowing,

but you, dear reader,

you are a bird-tree-Mad-human-person who doesn't need to know, because you feel it deep and hard. The feelers don't worry so much about knowing because the understanding reverberates and rests in our bodymindsouls. We become one with the despair and aching the same way we touch the freckles that dance across our sun-soaked skin and watch a doe tentatively turn her ears to the sound of crinkling leaves. The feelers understand this thing we call knowledge is always incomplete (Martusewicz, 2019). Feelers don't try to hold it tightly. To hold something so remarkable tightly would crush its bones and crumple its feathers.

This knowledge thing is not formal,

       rather it is something instantaneous and always present (Berry, 2002).

Knowledge is everywhere and all the time,

       coming from human people, red-breasted robins and winding ivy, jagged scars we wear, deep blue paints we smear across paper, the bond between Pigeon-cat and woman-bird, rich earthy soil and quiet rain, our togetherness and the bonds we share.

Yet, do not take my attachment to these shadowed parts as an indication that they are comfortable, palatable, or easy to bear. They are painful and sharp. They endure. For all the times being a feeler has beauty, it has teeth.

The teeth come as I stand in my kitchen, the illuminated stove clock casting an eerie witch's cauldron green across the room. It shifts. Numbers morphing on the digital screen, 1:00. It has to be one o'clock. Exactly. On. The. Dot.

No one tells you it will be like this.

No one tells you it might be standing in your kitchen, holding an ice cube to your stomach, the ice numbing your fingers as a droplet runs cold and wet down your prickled skin, before plunging in a needle. Then another. And a third.

> Hot tears streaming, not because it hurts
>> but because
>> it wasn't supposed to be like this.

But despair isn't just needles in kitchens.

It is an avalanche of heartaches and truths and untruths. It is a hurricane of over-truths, blood pouring from beating organs and bubbled flesh scalded and scarred that no one wants to hear or see. It's painful.

No.

Sometimes I lie.

To myself.

It isn't always painful. It isn't always teeth and gnashing bloodshed.

Sometimes despair is dull. And exhausted. It's achy and cavernous.

But I hold it gently, turn it in my hands tenderly, look at it longingly when I'm alone. I cup my hands around this small, delicate thing and am in awe of the mangled and imperfect wonder.

That's probably the thing most folks can't possibly understand.

> How something so indescribably hollow can be held so dear.

There's sad.

And then there's this.

Like a snowy lakeshore gust in the dead, dark night it howls through bones and tendons and bloody guts bringing me to my knees on the stairs. It smells like rusted metal and tightens around your neck.

Rough carpet against naked knees;

    it wasn't supposed to be like this.

A sound that I have never heard before, the most awful sound imaginable. Grating bone, shrieking birdcalls, grinding metal across pavement. I don't know where it comes from, somewhere eternal and somewhere dark. It's a desperate, hollow sound. A sound of a million women before me, the sisterhood I never wanted to be part of all speaking, screaming, crying, keening across the days, weeks, years. It is torrential, echoing from somewhere you didn't know existed. The cry is a sound that there are no words for and contains the pain of millennia and the pain of now all at once. Cascading, intensifying, and dying simultaneously, the calls of those before me and my own cries of desperation form each other. I crumple on my staircase and it escapes me and in this instant I know I will be screaming this guttural keen for all times.

I still hear it now.

I will never stop hearing it.

    I still hear it now.

    I still hear it now.

    I still feel it now,

        vibrating within me, below the surface.

How you can go on existing feeling so fucking empty.

    It's worse than sad,

        it's nothing.

        I retreat, quiet,

"We become less..." (Griffin, 1978, p. 28).

I resignedly beg the universe to take me,

to make me disappear.

I walk about in my human-woman suit pretending to be. I do what I think human people are supposed to do, even as my body-mindsoul aches and food turns to ash in my mouth. Despair rages through me—through *us* I suppose—and we don't know how to stop the machine, we strike ourselves just to feel. We scratch our wrists and slice open flesh. I question if I am a human-woman at all.

Fancy myself a tawny cardinal or a long—lashed doe,

quiet Dryopteris carthusiana, tentative Juniperus,

all-consuming and unrelenting fire,

or sunshine on your face on a cold day.

For, yes, *yes...*

The rabbit tracks in the yard whisper secrets,

the garden soil beneath her fingernails becomes her, and

"She can even, yes, hear what the birds say" (Griffin, 1978, p. 182).

"What if...

I feel like this forever?" I ask my therapist.

I've been promised by therapists of old that I have a broken brain,

a lifelong sickness (Whitaker, 2015).

I only ask her this because she isn't a knower, despite the credentials after her name. She is a feeler, like me. She has keened and hears it echoing still, yet somehow sits with me. Blunt-edged pale blonde hair and gently sloping shoulders. They are kind shoulders.

"What if...

it hurts like this forever?" I ask her.

Most of the time I think it will.

The next day, it is back to a doctor's office. It is snowing and

I grip the steering wheel with white knuckles. I imagine my car sliding across the expressway as I follow the curve of the road, the panic in my chest growing by the moment. While I drive, I listen to an audiobook and feel my stomach churn. I count the bracelets on my left wrist—each a string connecting me to the now-world. Each time I start to feel myself slipping away, I add another. Never take them off, stay safe and here and now. The bracelets keep me from going too far away.

Out of the car and up the stairs (123456123456), through the door to the silent waiting room. Sit in a chair with right angles. My index fingernail traces the white letters on a black rubber bracelet. I pull back an elastic beaded one so it snaps my pale inner wrist, burning. Wait for my name, don't look at the TV. Blood first. The woman who carefully slides the needle into my flesh is tender with kind eyes and always pats me gently. She never makes small talk. Even though we do this every day. For her unspoken tenderness, I am still grateful.

No one can tell me what is wrong, but they can tell me that the treatment isn't working. My body isn't responding, they say. I will my limbs and veins to do what they are supposed to. I beg my racing heart and stubborn bones to just do what I need them to. They ask me if I have more medicine at home and tell me to increase my dosage, see if it sets things in motion.

"Will we have to stop treatment if it doesn't?" I ask.

I am that patient who always asks too many questions. More than one doctor has commented on it. I am the patient who reads peer-reviewed journals and brings them to appointments. I make lists, exhaustive lists. Eventually after asking the first few questions I become insecure and stop asking. "That's all," I lie. You'd think this would show my commitment to understanding, but mostly it seems to just exhaust people. Most doctors don't welcome it. It makes them sigh.

"I don't have a crystal ball," the nurse snaps at me.

For her, this is another day at work. I'm just another woman in tears. For me, this is my life. For me, this is my body. For me, this is all-consuming and inescapable. We are not in the same storm.

Down the stairs of the doctor's office, 123456123456, I count, passing a woman in a puffy black coat. We don't make eye contact. It is another of the unwritten rules. Reaching the door, I head back out into the darkness. It is too early for even the sun to begin her crawl over the horizon. I have already driven an hour to have my body poked and prodded, now I drive another hour to work. My students will never know the tears that stream my face on my way. They don't know my arms are covered in a rainbow of bruises (some sallow yellow, others deep purple, one a sickly greenish hue) from the daily bloodwork. None of them see the blotchy welts and purple map of injections that splatters my torso.

I drive.

Winter, again. I was born in the winter and am one with the short days and deer tracks in the snow. In my youth, riding in the backseat I felt connected to the icy Michigan lakeshore that passed by my window. Blue ice erupting in jagged edges. Or, sometimes dark and smooth. Like the seasons of life and the waxing and waning of my Madness, the winter lake is inconsistent. Each form, curve, and edge haunting, beautiful, untamed. Even as a child I imagined what it must be like to drown beneath the ice.

Look up from underwater, the surface is black glass. Cold, dark, lake water in the middle of a wintery night. And you can't hear anything but the blood pulsing and beating in your ears. You know the quiet will come for you if you let it. It isn't melancholy. It is black glass. It is violent. And it is so empty.

How you can go on existing feeling so fucking empty.

It's worse than sad,

        it's nothing.

Whatever it is…. Whatever it is… I don't know or feel what it is… Whatever it is that makes it so painful, whatever it is that makes my despair so deep,

"It is always here, always becoming, always present.

It never goes away.

It doesn't know how.

And I wouldn't know what to do without it.

I don't know what to do without it" (Smith, 2018, p. 133).

I am no longer throwing away dishes, but the moments of pleasure are gone, too. Now instead of a green coat, there are more complex ways to hide. Professional competence, maintaining a fitness routine, and submitting my graduate school papers on time keep me free. Thirty-something cis-het white women are needed to be mothers and teachers. Even if I let down my guard, even if I stripped off my green coat and bared my bodymindsoul, I wonder if they would lock me up?

The green coat is in a box under the stairs. It's too big now. Or, I'm too small. Body collapsing into body, constricting into a smaller form. Pigeon got smaller, too. Smaller and smaller until we wrapped her in a towel each night and I had to poke her to keep well. Needles in stomachs and in bony furry cats. I will her to stay.

To stay here, I add another bracelet. This one rough stones and a metal clasp. I run fingers along it when I feel myself disappearing.

Stay here,
i will myself.
Stay now,
i will myself.

MadeMad ™

When I was young,
maybe six or seven,
    I thought we all

           found magic in mud on flesh,
           tenderly held frogs in our hands,
           wondered if sleep was dying,
           worried about being buried in a box,
           talked to barn cats with our eyes,
           climbed in pear trees and hid in forsythia bushes,
           repeated phrases over and over and over like in-
cantations for safety,
           hated ourselves for mixing up dimes and nickels
on a first grade test,
           picked flowers in the outfield of a baseball game,
              and carried deep despairs that made it
hard to breathe.

Now I consider that the racing thoughts, the endlessly dark nights, and the scratching fingernails across wrists was before I knew. Clinical checklists and person-first language would tell me that these characteristics are symptoms. Symptoms meet criteria. With the barn cats and in the forsythia, I never knew there were lists like that. Lists to describe thinking fast and feeling hard, counting, scratching, hiding, smiling. I wonder how they know what is DSM-5 worthy? What line separates a bird-human-woman-bodymind from the human-people who walk in their human-suits? Is the line thicker-than-thick, forged of steel and piled field rocks—is it huge, bigger than big, wider than wide, longer than long? Or is it a line as thin as the fibers that build a green coat, the point of a needle that stains ink on flesh, each gram you measure and count and tabulate before placing food on tongue?

Refuse the
risk of losing
        bird secrets and mud magic,
these parts
are interwoven roots on a forest floor.
Each nourishes me,
grounds me,
is me.
I am root,
        tree   needle sap
        nest   termite air
        snow   forest.
Three decades of learning
Made Mad™
                secrets—
wear the green coat
and talk to the birds.
cat-Pigeon and bird-woman,
        how long do I ask her to stay?
        how long do i make us stay?
We live (un)well because i don't know what else to do.
The living (un)well doesn't go away and it can't,
        it isn't past tense (Smith, 2018),
It sure won't get easier,
        it sure won't get easier.

i didn't let Pigeon-cat go,

    but she went.

    it didn't matter that i wanted her to stay.

The living doesn't and can't and won't get easier,

    maybe because it isn't supposed to.

IMPORTANT STUFF WORTH THINKING ABOUT

Adams, T. E. (2017) . Autoethnographic responsibilities. *International Review of Qualitative Research, 10*(1), 62-66.

Berry, W. (2002). Health is membership. In N. Wirzba (Ed.), *The art of the commonplace: The agrarian essays of Wendell Berry* (pp. 144-158). Berkeley, CA: Counterpoint.

Havas, M. (2008, June 5). Health concerns associated with Energy Efficient Lighting and their electromagnetic emissions. *Scientific Committee on Emerging and Newly Identified Health Risks (SCENIHR) Request for an Opinion on "Light Sensitivity"*, 11pp.

Griffin, S. (1978). *Woman and nature: The roaring inside her.* Berkeley, CA: Counterpoint.

Martusewicz, R. A., Edmundson, J., & Lupinacci, J. (2015). *EcoJustice education: Toward diverse, democratic, and sustainable communities.* New York, NY: Routledge.

Martusewicz, R. A. (2019). Love in the commons: Eros, eco-ethical education, and a poetics of place. In R. Foster, J. Makela, & R. A. Martusewicz (Eds.) *Art, EcoJustice, and Education: Intersecting Theories and Practices* (pp. 166-177). New York: Routledge.

Plath, S. (1981). Wintering. In T. Hughes (Ed.), *Sylvia Plath: The Collected Poems* (pp. 217-219). New York, NY: HarperCollins Publishers.

Plumwood, V. (2002). *Environmental culture: The ecological crisis of reason.* New York: Routledge.

Poole, J. M., & Ward, J. (2013). "Breaking open the bone": Storying, sanism, and mad grief. In B. A. LeFrancois, R. Menzies, & G. Reaume (Eds.) *Mad Matters: A Critical Reader in Canadian Mad Studies* (pp. 94—104). Toronto, ON: Canadian Scholars Press Inc.

Russo, J. (2016). Towards our own framework, or reclaiming madness part two. In J. Russo and A. Sweeney (Eds.), *Searching for a Rose Garden: Challenging Psychiatry, Fostering Mad Studies* (pp. 59-68). Monmouth: PCCS Books.

Smith, P. (2018). *Writhing writing: Moving towards a mad poetics.* Lexington, KY: Autonomous Press.

Starkman, M. (2013). The movement. In B. A. LeFrancois, R. Menzies, & G. Reaume (Eds.), *Mad Matters: A Critical Reader in Canadian Mad Studies* (pp. 27-37). Toronto: Canadian Scholars Press, Inc.

Whitaker, R. (2015). *Anatomy of an epidemic: Magic bullets, psychiatric drugs, and the astonishing rise of mental illness in America.* New York: Broadway Books.

Charleston Memorial

AUBRY THRELKELD

32°57'06"N 80°09'22"W   (EAGLE CREEK DRIVE ≈1986)

There used to be a palmetto tree in the front yard. Throughout the south the shoots of palmetto trees have been used as food, the leaves as bristles for cleaning, and the trees for decoration. Their trunks, just soft enough, absorbed cannonballs fired on Fort Moultrie at the start of the American Civil War. The fruits, resembling grapes, spring forth happily in summer, ripen, droop, and rot by late fall. The small concrete porch of the three-bedroom ranch house was positioned just far enough away from the tree that a child's running leap could not reach its fronds. Un-ironically, a birdbath sits where the palmetto once stood, concretely convinced of its own permanence. We moved in months after my parents' divorce, after briefly living with my Mom's best friend and her son.

I spent formative years on Eagle Creek Drive in Ladson, South Carolina, formerly my grandparents' home. Growing up there, the road was half paved and half dirt, and the backyard terraced down to the creek, where we lit contraband fireworks into the water and searched for Eocene whale bones and shark's teeth. I knelt into broken glass and still have the scar.

Behind the house a rustic, dusty shed stood where my grandfather made wine from muscadines and scuppernongs. The double, white-doored garage was always partly open, either for my brother's weightlifting routine, or later, for my mother's boyfriend's work on home improvements. It was a space for greeting my brother's friends passing in cars or bicycles. It was also a family forum: I discussed school from the steps inside as my mother washed clothes and my mother and brother got into more than one knock-down, drag-out fight there. Our dogs Mai Tai and later Pepper played in the garage and policed the backyard.

Across the street my mother's cousin and his wife Theresa lived in a two-story, split-level home. The tomb-like entryway to the house forced an immediate choice, up the stairs to the living area (den, kitchen, bathrooms, and bedrooms) or down to the master bedroom and garage. As a child, I went there often after school to play alongside my brother and my older cousin. But I was always more interested in Aunt Theresa, who I visited in the downstairs master bedroom.

She lay on a low-slung waterbed watching late afternoon soap operas or talk shows on an old boxy TV. A vanity where she put on her makeup had large, oversized, halogen lights, the kind you'd see in the movies. To the left of the door was a walk-in-closet—my childhood definition of decadent luxury—replete with sequined gowns in red, white, and blue—and high heels on the floor for easy access, some upright and others knocked over. By afternoon light, filtered through trees, shined through mirrored insets on the walls, Aunt Theresa always shared her makeup and her clothes with me. I sneaked into her closet to touch her dresses or sometimes swipe a brownish garnet-toned lipstick.

32°54'24.4"N 79°59'52.3"W   (INVERNESS LANE <1985)

Here were my earliest memories. I had a blue bedroom in the back of what was my paternal grandparent's house, with bookshelves and a toy crate. The three-bedroom house sat atop what felt like, to a small child riding a tricycle, a really tall hill. Brick columns flanking the driveway had a brass sign that read Threlkeld. Later, as an adolescent living in nearby North Charleston, I drove by them and thought about chipping away at the brick at night to remove the sign—a misguided dream of reclaiming a lost family connection. My bedroom held traumatic memories; the house held more. Sometimes, my parents closed the door while they fought. When that happened, I couldn't leave the room.

The house had a voluminous den with a sliding glass door; pill bugs accumulated in the door's tracks. The family dog loved to run in and out the door into the backyard. My mother lived in the kitchen, washed dishes, and cooked.

My father lost his own father as a young adult. They hunted deer together and loved each other immensely. My father dropped out of high school, addicted to alcohol, and later other substances—likely cocaine when he could afford it.

One fall night in 1986 it all came to a violent end. My father came home high and attacked my mother. He was often verbally abusive and neglectful, but this was something different. I heard crashes from my blue bedroom. My brother, whose room sat next to mine, came in and said I needed to stay put. A few moments later my mother—drenched in tears, bruised, and beaten—came in and said we needed to go. She hurriedly got me into a jacket; she was injured but I don't remember how. I wore pajamas and grabbed my stuffed Big Bird. My mother hurried us down the hall, through the living room, and onto the front porch, my father following quickly behind. My mother reassured us, said we'd be ok. My father hit my brother who tried to defend us, earning him a cut on his forehead. It would become a recurring theme. Looking up at my crazed father's face, I asked if I could have my shoes—I wasn't supposed to be outside without my shoes on, and didn't want to do anything wrong.

My father said, simply, "No."

We walked about a mile to the nearest pay phone at the Hot Spot gas station and called my mother's best friend. She picked us up.

32°49'13.0"N 80°02'07.8"W   (DAD'S APARTMENT ≈ 1988)

My mother's boyfriend shot her other boyfriend, Greg, while I was staying with my father. My mother had been dating both of them at the same time. It made it into the newspapers and the television. The first boyfriend pleaded self-defense. He also went to high school with the District Attorney.

I spent more time with my father than usual. During the struggle, when Greg crushed my brother behind a refrigerator, my mother's boyfriend feared for his life and the safety of my mother. So, he shot and killed him. I really liked Greg. His family called our house for years after his death. I was instructed to not answer the phone. My mother's boyfriend started carrying a pistol with him everywhere. He loves the Second Amendment.

32°53'43"N 80°28'42"W   (HARMONY HALL LANE ≈ 1988)

The short dirt road opened off the highway by a tall oak tree dripping with Spanish moss, and led to a spot where a brown double wide trailer used to sit. A wooden unfinished deck greyed by the Southern heat marked where my grandmother used to sit and listen to Eastern whip-poor-wills sing while she smoked her Winstons. She might play old country music, listen to the drone of a large console television, or ask me, in singsong cadence, "How much do I love you?" Our answer, always rehearsed, spoken together, and sometimes choreographed: "How deep is the ocean? How high is the sky?" These lyrics (from a song written by Irving Berlin) bonded us after my uncle Johnny died in a motorcycle accident: going too fast trying to avoid being late to work. The words opened up conversation and simultaneously said goodbye.

Sitting behind the brown mobile home was a chicken coop, a crumbling building for tools and a deer freezer. Later, it was joined by a tin-clad garage for an old boat without a plug for drainage (we know because it sank), and a rusty tractor outfitted with a tiller. Little of this remains in the Google Earth satellite images I can see today. I can still make out the house and trees overtaking the shed.

I started to have flashbacks as a child from eight to about sixteen. They started after I was raped in the woods two hundred yards or so behind the shed, in a tree stand, by my brother. It happened during one of the short summer trips my brother and I took to visit my grandparents. I cried out in the woods. My brother told me to shut up, that no one would hear me.

I looked down from the tree stand to the pine forest floor. I didn't want to stand up. I didn't want to go back to my grandparents' house. As I stumbled back, I noticed the deer feed my grandfather had planted drying in the soil under the hot Carolina sun.

Looking at Google aerial photographs, you can see the scale of development in rural South Carolina, once farmland, but now mostly pine forest plantations for paper mills dotting the coast. I can't see the tree stand anymore, or the plowed field where my grandfather lured deer for hunting. I know my estranged uncle lives just a few hundred feet from the clearing.

Those pine forests, once protected as part of a state forest system, bustle with rural development. House after house collects water into pools and ponds. The aerial view shows paved roads where there were once only dirt lanes. Maybe the small creek where my grandfather illegally shot an alligator is a water treatment plant. Our nearest neighbors, the Bryant family, who grew sugarcane, watermelons, and all kinds of vegetables alongside the swampy road, have a fresh coat of paint on their house. Their garden is gone. Their children must have sold the property or taken it over after they died of cancer. The house was yellow. Now it's green. I read Rimbaud there.

32°57'06"N 80°09'22"W   (EAGLE CREEK DRIVE ≈1986)

After school, my cousin, brother, and I stopped by Aunt Theresa's house. The stairs into the house were unusually steep for me; my brother and cousin led the way. We walked into a living horror film.

My cousin found her first. Then my brother. Then me. I crawled up the beige, carpeted stairs to discover Aunt Theresa had shot herself in the head. The shot hadn't killed her outright, however, and she was still alive when we found her. She spent a while bleeding out before we arrived, semi-conscious, trying to put herself back together. She laid out clothes. She wandered through the large atmospheric living room. She stood in the upstairs bathroom covered in her own blood applying makeup to herself.

I peered into the kitchen and the living room. I could smell the iron in the warm blood. I stood up and froze in place. The trails of blood in the carpet, indelible in my mind, serve me still as a way to distance myself from what I know I saw: beautiful Aunt Theresa, now a corpse. My brother picked me up and screamed at me to stay outside of the house. I spent what felt like hours sitting on the wooden porch staring through slats while we waited for parents and police.

Police arrived eventually. My cousin Joe—who I called Uncle Joe—changed and would never be the same. The light drained from his face; his cheeks sagged. Drug use was rumored to have precipitated Theresa's suicide. Some said her depression caused it all. My brother went into counseling; so did my cousin. My brother told my mother I saw nothing; he probably believes it still. My mother was distraught.

I don't remember ever crossing the street again. I would look up at the house from my bicycle like it had somehow changed. If I felt brave I did fast loops in the circle driveway and speed off down the street, feeling Theresa's spirit at my back.

For weeks after the suicide, I kept my nightlight on in my room, my way of warding off bad thoughts. It didn't work. I kept having visions of my Aunt Theresa. At one point I remember her touching my arm and saying, "I'm going to be ok, baby." Except she wasn't. Clotted blood leaked from the hole in her head. Her touch, cold and wet, chilled me to the bone. I began to construct elaborate forts out of stuffed animals sure that no inch of my body stuck out so I wouldn't have to feel her touch again. I heard her rummage through my room. I asked for a brighter light bulb for my nightlight. It was so hot it melted the red balloons carried by the clown. At some point it became a joke in the family: "Why does Aubry still need a nightlight?"

32°54'46.0"N 80°01'23.9"W   (LUCILLE DRIVE ≈ 1991)

I always asked my teachers if I could sit in a corner of the classroom. Being there was solace. I knew who was approaching me. I could see the abuse coming. My brother went off to military school, thank God... I felt strong and knew if I was in the corner, I could depend on my own strength and fight back.

I felt the same about being in a rudimentary fort in the backyard of my mother's partner's house. Cats, birds, and rats roamed the brush behind the fence. Our neighbor, an older white woman, fed the cats and spent a lot of time manicuring her lawn. I concocted potions in empty cans, pretending I was a wizard who could change the world through a mixture of dirt, water, and ferment. I didn't have friends except for people I talked to at the bus stop.

I lived almost exclusively in my room. I did homework night after night, sinking into academic achievement as a way to get attention and praise. I had flashbacks of being raped by my brother, but I recited a mantra to push them away, thinking that I would just die with this knowledge, and that if I cried enough about it the pain could disappear: "What if my grandmother died. What if my dog died. What if my mother died. What if I died." I said this every night over and over again for a couple of years until I didn't cry when I said it.

My father gave me a stereo as a kind of apology for not being around, and I listened to the radio all night. I danced and sang when I felt despair. If the day was right, I could catch Suzanne Vega's song, *Luka*. Somehow it captured my abuse story, especially the lyric, "Just don't ask me what it was."

32°57'06"N 80°09'22"W   (EAGLE CREEK DRIVE ≈1986-9)
It started when my brother invited me to masturbate him in the shower. He told me I could do it to myself, too, and that it was fun. I believed everything he said. He had protected me and my mother. He had saved me from drowning once while we were on vacation in Mexico Beach, Florida with our grandparents.

The masturbation moved to his bedroom and he started what I would later learn was called a grooming process. He told me that I could never tell anyone what we did because they would take me away from my family and that my mother would go to prison. I was so scared my mother was going to be taken away that I followed her around when she returned home from work. Masturbation turned to oral sex.

Then, after my brother took intercrural intercourse too far, he forced himself on me. I screamed and cried. He told me it would be ok, that I just needed to relax. It felt like my insides were wrenched from me. I hovered above my body, somehow was not even there, a traumatic astral projection. The makeshift gun rack in my brother's room rattled like a deathknell. I had an impaction, and my mother had to help me defecate. My brother stood outside the door to the bathroom staring me down, worried that I might slip and tell her what happened.

I was raped perhaps 25 times before I was 10 years old. I thought that playing hide-and-seek meant that I would be raped. I asked my brother if anyone had ever touched him the way he touched me. He responded proudly, "Yes, of course, I had a babysitter who used to touch me. It was great." I started to expect pain when going about my daily life.

42°21'05.9"N 71°08'34.3"W   (CAMBRIDGE AVE ≈ 2021)

The COVID-19 pandemic had me revisiting places I hadn't seen in decades via Google Earth Street View. I wrote down memories to connect my madness to space through time. They documented a variety of strategies I used to distance myself from my family and life history. Since I couldn't travel I dreamt of traveling, remembering places that I often flashback to, or places where I have hallucinated. These flashbacks and hallucinations were precipitated simply by moving or transitioning to a new place. Now I can see these places both for what they are and for what they were. In my accumulated memories they meld. Madness was and perhaps will always be a blending of worlds.

Remembering is looking through my life story(s) bespeckled. There are blind spots where everything is hazy, and other moments of intense clarity heightened by the inability to see the whole picture. I've probably filled in the gaps since I can't remember everything. This text is an archive before I forget to remember again.

My best friend read this and told me that she never heard all these stories. I don't remember not telling her. I just assumed everyone knew. I just assumed that when I was in therapy—which was a really long time—everyone heard me.

I imagine my Aunt Theresa looked like Gia Carangi, the bisexual 80's supermodel who died of AIDS. Even my mother's cousin Joe has now passed.

My mother's other boyfriend Greg was so kind to me. He was a bodybuilder and always made me feel welcome. He gave her a jewelry box that sat on her dresser for a long time: a memorial without a dedication. It took me years to forgive my stepfather and to recognize his anger and need for therapy. I brought up the jewelry box when I wanted to start a fight.

32°57'06"N 80°09'22"W   (EAGLE CREEK DRIVE ≈1989)

I thought I was dying of AIDS because I had been raped by my brother. I told all of my friends in elementary school I wouldn't be back next year. I figured everyone would find out when I died. In my queer 1980's drama, I was Ryan White and Judith Light played my mother. I wrote singsong poetry about my own death.

32°56'00.2"N 80°02'27.5"W   (DUNLAP STREET ≈ 1991-1993)

My father, his new girlfriend, and her family lived in Summit Place Apartments before they moved to Goose Creek. At the time, I visited when it was just my father there, though three kids and two adults shared a two-bedroom apartment. The apartment buildings, largely grey and modular, gave a feeling both of privacy and community. In the center of the complex was a pool, a changing room, and a hot tub shared by all of the residents.

One summer night I was excited to go to the pool. I could swim but it was really important that I was accompanied, so my "cousin" as I called him (he was the son of my father's girlfriend) came with me. We played in the pool for a while, and I practiced diving. I remember my cousin not being particularly engaged. He spent most of his time in the hot tub. Longing for some social contact, I jumped in the hot tub with him and talked about video games. I had recently discovered role-playing video games and tried to get everyone I know interested in the games. My cousin and I had played these together many times.

The conversation shifted. He asked me if I could see what was happening under water in the hot tub. I naively responded no, that I didn't have my glasses on. He told me to dive under water and look. So, I did. He was masturbating. A flood of emotions overwhelmed me. I had flashbacks talking to him. I needed to get out of the hot tub, but didn't want to anger or alert my cousin that his sexual advances were unwelcome. I told him that I knew what he was doing, and I wasn't interested. He pressed me further. He begged. He said if I could just put my hand or mouth on him, he'd feel better. He'd feel less alone.

I continued to say I wasn't interested, that I needed to go back to the apartment. He said that he would come along. I could see him hard in his bathing shorts as he followed me into the changing room. I started to take my clothes off; he approached me and pulled down his shorts. I screamed and said that I didn't want him to touch me. He backed away. I swung a towel at him and told him he was disgusting. For the first time I felt powerful. Here was another man trying to rape me, just like my brother. I told him if he got close to me ever again, I was going to tell everyone that he was a pervert and liked touching children.

I pulled my swimsuit back on and ran back to the apartment without him. I stood for a moment next to the yellow day lilies beside the apartment entrance, debating whether or not to tell my father about what happened. In the apartment, my father sat on the overstuffed sofa watching sports on television. He asked where my cousin was and why I was wearing my swimsuit. I did not want to get in trouble myself; I told him I left because I was bored and that I preferred changing at home. I lied. I never went back into my cousin's room alone. He avoided me. I felt powerless and powerful.

33°84'N, 81°16'W   (EAST HOME AVENUE ≈ 1997)

I woke up with nightmares again. The scene of being raped by my brother in the tree stand played over and over in my head. Other flashbacks (I called them daydreams) included memories of hiding from my brother behind a houndstooth jacket in the coat closet on Eagle Creek Drive so he couldn't ask me to "play." Sometimes I felt numb, other times paralyzed, and sometimes I just cried. On too many nights I stared at the wall and zoned out for hours at a time. I also felt a strong surge of adolescent yearning. I didn't know if it was wrong to touch myself, or experience pleasure of any kind. I would masturbate, stop, and cry. Years before, my brother had assured me, while driving my grandfather's blue truck down a dirt road, that if I ever told anyone, he would kill me, or that I would be taken away from my family. That no longer felt true. He moved to Missouri to work for the police, married, reconnected to his father, had children, and I didn't even go home for weekends anymore.

My mother married my stepfather while I was away at school. I wasn't invited to the wedding. I think my mother knew I had objections, yet we never had a chance to talk through them. I didn't know if I could forgive my new stepfather for killing a man. My father had recently left rehab and he had a renewed interest in my life. I began to lose contact with my grandparents.

I lived full time at a residential school over 45 minutes away from my home. I knew I needed to tell someone about what happened to me. I had rape flashbacks during my pre-calculus class. Trigonometry was baffling; I only ever got part of the equation, leaving me staring blankly at triangles with Greek letters set beside them. When my teacher, Mrs. Rutherford, called on me, I just expected to get the answer somehow wrong. I dreaded being asked to explain my answer when I could barely remember where I was.

I became obsessed with Maya Angelou's writings. I had read *I Know Why the Caged Bird Sings* twice over the summer before my junior year of high school. For the first time, I learned about the powerful role rape and incest had in silencing me. I didn't know where to start to get help.

For two days in a row, I walked over to the guidance counselor's office. I didn't go in, just waved. I said kind words to the administrators. I walked away. Repeat. Finally, I knew I had to ask for help and utter the words out loud. I wrote a script: "I was a victim of incest and rape. I need help. I can't hold it in anymore." I spoke to a guidance counselor, Gerald. He made me repeat my script. I'm not sure he initially believed it. Later, Gerald drove me to Florence to see a therapist. The therapist listened to my rape and abuse history. I also told the therapist that I was bisexual and that I was afraid that my sexuality related to my abuse. He disabused me of the latter. He did say that if I was bisexual that I would never be happy unless I chose to be either gay or straight. I started telling people that I was gay to avoid questions.

32°47'02.7"N 79°56'16.0"W   (COLLEGE OF CHARLESTON≈1999)

I stood in front of an auditorium of college students and told my story. I said that I identified as queer and that I was a survivor of rape and incest. It was the first time I spoke out as a survivor of abuse. The whole moment flashed before me. I was acting as a youth intern at We Are Family, a local queer-youth support group. Ever so briefly, I was one of their first youth board members, and traveled to queer conferences like Creating Change in Oakland and later in Atlanta which shaped my identity for years to come.

44°00'32.6"N 73°10'45.5"W   (MIDDLEBURY COLLEGE ≈ 2000)

Aunt Theresa came with me to college. She opened the door to my room and peered in. She asked if I was ok. I wasn't. I didn't feel like I belonged so far from home. Chris, a new friend, came and slept on the floor beside my bed for a week. I painted an effigy of my aunt and hung it on my wall. I placed a cross on it.

42°22'19.8"N 71°07'08.7"W   (HARVARD SQUARE ≈ 2008)

Right after I started a doctoral program in education at Harvard, I was diagnosed with C-PTSD. The list of associated concerns/ characteristics was exhausting: hypervigilance/hyperarousal, agoraphobia, bulimia, panic attacks, anxiety, depression, and relationship difficulties. My Madness—told through medicalized language—interacted with my experience with arthritis, chronic pain, sleep, and a general inability to trust. I moved through my own Mad world where every aspect of my life was filtered through my bodymind's experience of trauma, abuse, and the lifelong effects of not receiving treatment earlier.

Maybe it was inevitable: my grandmother was depressed; my grandfather was an abusive alcoholic and womanizer; my mother was depressed and hospitalized multiple times; my father was an abusive alcoholic who needed rehab to even come back into my life; and my uncle never recovered from the Vietnam War, coping with the aftereffects of death and symptoms of Agent Orange exposure. My uncle had C-PTSD too—also diagnosed late. My brother had been abused himself. He was later charged with statutory rape, and his family split up after he was accused of abusing his daughter. At least one of my cousins accused him of rape. I know at least two other people he abused who have never told their stories: neither is doing well. I feel safe because I can always look him up geographically through Megan's Law (even while disagreeing with surveillance laws).

I've come to understand the ways that routine rape breaks down your will to live and connect with others. I realized that I'd been disassociating for a long while, and that I had been living in multiple worlds, never fully in any. Doctors talked to me about hospitalization.

42°23'45.3"N 71°07'15.6"W   (DAVIS SQUARE ≈ 2009)

After it became clear that my partner of seven years and I were breaking off our engagement, I knew my flashbacks and hallucinations would come back. It made me angry at my partner—not because our relationship was ending, which I agreed with—but precisely because I didn't want to face the paralysis again. I had to be better by now, right? I wrestled with the idea that mental illness was a permanent state. I froze. In one week, I needed a place to live.

My mother flew up from Charleston and helped me move into a storage unit. She brought her best friend. They did all the work. I cried every time I tried to pack my belongings. Everything reminded me of the life I built to escape my past. I feared I would be at the mercy of my mental illness, that my life would be forever shaped by where I came from. I sought therapy again, but not before hallucinations came back.

Aunt Theresa walked into the bedroom I had once shared. She stood at the door in a light dress drenched in her blood and talked to me. She asked if I was ok. The blood on her clotted and leaked. She touched my arm as I sat upright in bed. I could feel her blood on my body. She came five times in seven days. I beat my hands against the pine hardwood floors until they bled. I had hoped that I could have a relationship that would last. I didn't understand I couldn't make that happen by sheer force of will.

I needed a distraction from my hallucinations. In the breakup I lost contact with a large number of our mutual friends. I sought true online friendships through OkCupid and Craigslist. I knew I could not manage another relationship with someone, but I also knew I could not spend all of my time alone working. I no longer believed that all work was good and necessary. It was hard to focus. I met a young man around my age, also pursuing his doctorate. I made it clear that I was only interested in talking. We talked about a lot of things, but the last thing he told me was that had studied as a Haitian Vodou priest. A white American himself, he told me about the white racist fantasies of voodoo; he swept me away with some of the most fascinating stories I had ever heard. We met for Tibetan food around the corner from my apartment.

I told him about my hallucinations and how counseling and psychotropic medications helped lessen their severity, though their persistence concerned me. He told me I was lucky. He said, "Aubry, you have Dead. Some people spend their whole lives trying to commune with the dead, understand them, and never achieve that. This is a gift. You are in control." He described a ritual I could perform. I took notes as he spoke. I asked clarifying questions. I needed a candle and a picture of her or something that reminded me of her. I needed to tell her what I wanted from her. Maybe he made the whole thing up for my benefit. I think he's from the Midwest. I don't know, our friendship didn't last.

But he gave me something everlasting; he ministered to me. I adapted the ritual he described with some poetry I had written to her and I burned a candle through the night. She came again. Instead of being paralyzed, I asked her why she cared so much about how she looked in life, but wouldn't take care of herself in death. Aunt Theresa told me, "I come to see you because I love you. I want you to be happy and I know you are hurting." I told her that she hurt me when she didn't bother putting on her makeup and her best clothes. She uttered through tears, "I never meant to hurt you."

37°45'31.5"N 122°24'56.2"W?   (SAN FRANCISCO ≈ 2009)

I flew across the country to stay with my friend Chris. He had stayed by my side when I hallucinated in college and provided comfort then. We walked the length of the city. My legs ached. We ate Chinese style Dungeness crab and laughed.

The Castro Theater hosted a Moulin Rouge-themed sing-along and I sat next to Chris's friend who belted out songs the whole time.

He cried at the end. I held him. He asked me why I wasn't moved by the movie's themes of sickness, love, and loss. I replied cryptically, "I wish I hadn't taught myself not to cry." I didn't even know how to flirt without being self-deprecating. A few nights later, after telling him I was of Roma descent, he sang *Gypsy* by Fleetwood Mac to me. We kissed passionately. I ignored the racism.

He took me to Martuni's where we downed Manhattans and met a Vietnamese-American drag king who performed Sinatra tunes and was looking for a drag name. Someone suggested Rick Shaw. The performer thought it fit perfectly. I fantasized about skipping my flight back to Boston and starting a life between the Mission and the Castro.

I wrote a lot of poetry. I told Chris that when I'm in California I like to go to the ocean. We took a bus to a train to get to the Pacific Ocean. It took forever to get there. We stood looking over the water on a cliffside and down at the rocks below. I remember thinking: it's late, we'd better get back.

Mad Out Loud

DEVIN S. TURK

The translucent pill boxes. The laminated hospital bracelets. The safety levels. The strip-search. All the hours spent staring at the carpet in therapy offices, trying to justify my life through words that don't feel like they fit right. These things have *happened to me*. Even now, grasping at gut feelings and wisps of my memory to form these words is like trying to capture the vastness of the ocean in a bucket. I have been articulating myself over and over to what feels like little avail. I tell curious and well-meaning people that "no, those aren't my pronouns" or "actually, I *am* Autistic." I explain, explain, explain that referring to me as "high functioning" is an ableist aggression (before attempting to teach people what the word "ableist" means), that I am neither a man nor a woman, and that many things in my life—from my gender to my medical history—are "kind of a long story." I explain, rinse, and repeat in conversations with friends old and new, with family, with strangers, and with health professionals. I noticed this cycle of articulation first with my transness, then my Autism, followed by the reckoning of such a combination. Now, finally, I see this urgency embedded in my quest to articulate something I have come to know as "Madness."

Much of the way we as a culture talk about how distress is treated signals acceptance of a linear kind of timeline, a trajectory that aims toward "recovery" from an ailment. Generally speaking, the narrative of sickness is that the sick seek *help*, and that *help* makes the sickness *better*. Professional intervention disappears the chaos of illness, or so many of us assume. In my opinion, to "recover" implies the resumption of some kind of idealized "before" state, an existence before the onset of otherness. But if I have no "before," then what am I to recover? I was *born* an Autistic; a neuro-queer Sensitive inclined toward Madness in response to a world—with its abrasive bustle and lack of sameness—which is not suited to a bodymind like mine. I cannot "recover" what never was, but this is not the tragedy. The tragedy exists in the negative space; the tragedy exists in how we as a culture do *not* address *dynamics* of Madness.

One might dismiss the following discourse as a game of semantics, but I remain confident that our word choices matter. Do I *have* mental illnesses? Am *I* mentally ill? Do I embody illness, sickness, disorder? If I am "mentally ill," I wonder exactly which *parts* of me are sick. Does my illness lie embedded in my neurological structure? Does it come alive with the intensity of my emotional states? Am I disordered because of the ways I behave...or *mis*behave? Who is determining what qualifies as misbehavior? Through posing these questions, I have discovered the alternative frameworks of thinking that inform the Mad movement. Combined with my growing knowledge of the overlapping Autistic self-advocacy and disability justice movements, I am starting to form stronger opinions about what it means and doesn't mean to have a psychiatric diagnosis, to be a long-term mental patient, to be someone who hurts too much and wants the pain to go away. It turns out, I've found, that just wanting to be rid of extreme emotional distress is extraordinarily complicated.

Between the ages of fourteen and twenty-two, I spent a collective eighteen months in psychiatric treatment programs. During the same timeframe, beginning in my early teen years, I was prescribed a varied list of two dozen different psychiatric medications, often five or more at a time, up to three times per day, in attempt to contain my unruly despair. I cried a lot. I didn't have any close friends. I had panic attacks and sometimes dug my fingernails into my flesh to cope. The prescriptions for pills piled up, one after another. One psychiatrist I visited for a second opinion made the observation that my experience with psychiatric treatment appeared to be like "throwing spaghetti at a wall to see if it sticks," which I now find both humorous and horrifying. Some of my medications triggered allergic reactions or elicited bizarre side effects like extreme sensitivity to light or body convulsions. Most of the medications, though, blend together in my memory as being largely ineffective. I couldn't and still can't tease apart the effects of one drug from the effects of the next, which was compounded by the fact that I was on so many of them at any given time. Of course, I don't know where I'd be (or even *if* I'd be) if I had not begun taking medication, but from time to time, I wonder. Would I be different? Would that difference be "better" than my life now? Again, what does "better" mean, anyway?

As a years-long psychiatric consumer, I was—and to some degree, still am—so desperate to escape misery, no wonder I took every pill I was prescribed. Being a patient isn't much of a choice when it's the only choice you have. What if what I needed most wasn't an ever-changing cocktail of drugs and safety checks every fifteen minutes, but rather the feeling of peace in my own skin and the comfort of having good friends to count on? I have no easy answer. It was simpler, after all, for adults to instruct my younger self to swallow a benzodiazepine after a meltdown and sleep off the panic than it would have been to help me along in discovering my own identities, in beginning my gender transition, in maintaining a first meaningful friendship with a peer based on mutual understanding. I don't blame myself. I am instead growing critical of this system, this industry, which all too often seems to not acknowledge its own faults.

It baffles me that the science—perhaps the *art*—of prescribing psychiatric medication is one that seems to lean so heavily into chance. When I went to the doctor with a simple infection, I was prescribed an antibiotic to clear it up. After taking the pills as prescribed, the infection subsided, and my symptoms disappeared. My emotional distress—along with the distress of countless people like me—is nothing like having Strep Throat, but these wildly differing cases are funneled through the same Medical Model of Disability. Feeling too much can be a symptom. So can scratching at your arms until you begin to bleed. Avoiding eye contact is a symptom. Hell, *avoiding anything* itself can be classified as a symptom. Many of these parts of my life—these "symptoms" of mine—arose out of the conflict between my inherent neurotype and a world of deeply ableist and saneist power structures. These traits and behaviors are not merely purposeless symptoms of sickness or displays of psychopathology; they are harm reduction tactics, damage control, and a means of self-protection. But they have been medicalized, even vilified, so I am expected to work toward being rid of them. I am supposed to tell a nurse when I am thinking of scratching at my arm. I am supposed to surrender anything I could use to hurt myself. I am supposed to catalog my feelings, write them down, rate them on a scale of one to ten. I'm supposed to take all of my pills exactly as prescribed by my physician. Supposed to, supposed to, supposed to...

Right now, I remain very much "in the system" as a psychiatric consumer. Moreover, I have long embodied the trope of the so-called "good patient" since entering into the system as a child. A "good patient" exemplifies the narrative of the ideal consumer who is willing to abide by doctor's orders; it is someone who exhibits gentle compliance and doesn't ask too many questions or make objections. As a result, "good patients" are met with praise and trust. In psych hospitals, "good patients" don't have their outside time or phone privileges revoked. Consumers who fail at being "good patients" often lose their right to privacy, bodily autonomy, or some combination of the two. The thing is, the "good patient" is both a reality and a false construct. Nobody is inherently or ethically "good" or "bad" at being a patient or services consumer. Rather, these narratives are constructed around us and then plastered upon us. Being one of the "good" patients has served me well, to a certain end. I report symptoms and feelings, I gauge my own safety and promise not to seriously harm myself, I show up to every therapy appointment on time, and I take my meds. I am *compliant*. Even when I was fourteen on an inpatient psychiatric unit, I saw that this kind of behavior was a gateway. Because of my compliance, I was *allowed* to go down to the cafeteria for mealtimes, I was *allowed* ten minutes of phone time at the end of the day to call my mom and dad. And, after the minimum length of stay, I was *allowed* to walk out of the locked doors and return to my life...all because I was one of the "good" ones. Every now and then, I have nightmares about being one of the "bad" psych patients. I would say more specifically that I have nightmares about being a psych patient *whose autonomy and self-determination are compromised*, but I figure that right now, to me, being a psych patient has been inherently linked with compromised autonomy and obstructed self-determination. In the nightmares, I'm trying to escape a locked ward only to find that the elevator is broken, or I'm lying on a gurney, pleading with figures hovering over me who threaten me with injectable sedatives. I am begging, begging, begging to be believed. Then, I wake up.

It goes without saying that behind each doctoral degree is a flesh-and-blood human being. Every single person who walks into a psychiatrist's office is, in fact, a person. But only one of those people has the prescription pad. Only one of those people wears the white lab coat. Only one of those people is taking notes, conducting analysis, and, importantly, receiving payment from the other. Only one of those people, depending on the setting, can have the other ordered to be locked in an empty, padded room or physically or chemically restrained against their will. For these reasons, (as well as many more nuanced factors) the relationship between a psychiatrist and the person seated on the couch across from them is unequal in its balance of power. This differential is one major aspect of being a psychiatric consumer that I think is underdiscussed outside of the Mad movement. I have experienced a striking lack of personally satisfying discussions about this power imbalance with people who aren't patients, consumers, or survivors of psychiatric treatment or abuse. This is not at all to say that medical doctors are generally incapable of non-harmful participation in such conversations. I do believe, however, that holding conscious space for the consequences of the doctor-patient power differential to be properly acknowledged and explored takes a seasoned knowledge of interpersonal and systemic power intricacies, as well as a thorough understanding of how and why power differentials have been historically weaponized against vulnerable populations.

When I try to articulate what it has been like for me to have been a long-term psychiatric patient, I find myself tripping over my words. It feels, in a way, parallel to the desperation I felt during the extreme mental states that accompanied the Serotonin Syndrome I experienced at fourteen. A whirlwind mixture of fear and anger; a deep-rooted wariness of (and also a frantic pressure to appease) authority figures borne out of my being tricked into powerlessness. Beginning to think critically about the mental "health" system has been like opening a kind of Pandora's Box. I have tapped into an array of knowledge and emotions about what I have experienced, as well as a growing vocabulary I can use to articulate myself. Trying to put all of this into words is difficult and complicated and tiring. I know what I have to say may cause others to disagree with me, which is scary. But when I wake up each morning and take my medications with a growing sense of disillusionment; when I leave yet another therapist's office after an unsatisfactory session; when I toss and turn at night thinking of everything I've been through and where it has and has not led me, *I* am the only one who lives with the feeling that follows. So, I have come to the conclusion that however tedious or tiring the process may be, I need to speak and share more about how I experience my own bodymind and the consequences of living a life like mine in the midst of an ableist, saneist world. I need to be *Mad out loud*. To be Mad out loud means I must work in the direction of a Mad identity that is political in addition to deeply personal. It means listening to my intuition, and it means valuing the sound of my own voice even when it speaks alone. I anticipate that this will be an arduous process which will last not only for the duration of my lifetime, but long after. Here, I am thinking of the generations of people just like me who were—and continue to be—lost to a system which, however well-intentioned, has in many ways replicated the very harm and disfunction it has aimed to treat. I am thinking of icepick lobotomies. I am thinking of the countless queer survivors and non-survivors of conversion therapy. Scores of nameless headstones marking the final resting places of the restless on the grounds of abandoned asylums. Autistic children whose joy and communication are shushed with "quiet hands." People whose freedom, bodily autonomy, and dignity may or may not be returned to them after seventy-two hours. I am Mad out loud for them. I am Mad out loud for us.

about the editor

Phil Smith is completely post-everything—he is SO after that. formerly a big deal perfesser guy, with teaching gigs in vermont, michigan, and illinois, he slipped disability and mad studies cranky rants into courses he taught. at eastern michigan university, as a full professor, he was director of the brehm center for special education scholarship and research, and head of the department of special education. phil received the 2002 vermont crime victim service award, the emerging scholar award in disability studies in education in 2009, and the eastern michigan university college of education innovative scholarship award in 2015.

his writing—academic and creative—has been published widely, since 1977. phil has had 60 papers published in a buncha different journals, *including Disability Studies Quarterly, Taboo, Rural Special Education Quarterly, Qualitative Inquiry, Intellectual Disabilities; Review of Educational Research,* and *Health and Place. he's* published a whole lotta book chapters, and made over 120 presentations and keynote addresses in local, state, national, and international venues.

he studied creative writing at a couple of universities, as well as photography, filmmaking, and education. a poet, playwright, novelist, and visual and performance artist, his creative books include *pomes; plaze; hagiography, or the electron; hats; keweenaw bay songs; landscapes; machines; doors and walls and windows; still life; the reach; this place is north; poems come;* and *cutting wood.*

phil describes himself azza critical scholar and a whatever-comes-after-qualitative researcher. his academic work includes two books exploring disability studies, *Whatever Happened to Inclusion? The Place of Students with Intellectual Disabilities in Education* and *Both Sides of the Table: Autoethnographies of Educators Learning and Teaching With/In [Dis]ability;* as well as a textbook entitled, *Disability and Diversity: An Introduction.* his book, *writhing writing: moving towards a mad poetics,* won the 2020 American Educational Studies Association Critics Choice Award.

for more than 25 years, in a variety of contexts and roles, he worked as a disability and mad rights activist, and served on the boards of directors of a number of regional, state and local organizations, including the Society for Disability Studies, where he was President.

he's mad (but not, mostly, angry) as hell, a walkie, and identifies as disabled. a life-long Yankee, he lived for a coupla decades in michigan, spending as much time as he could beside Lake Superior, where loons, wolves, moose, and bald eagles peeked in the windows of his cabin. now he lives on the side of a mountain at 1800 feet, in an even smaller cabin, fussing and ranting with his tree and animal neighbors.

about the authors

Jenn Layton Annable is a Mad, Neurodivergent, genderqueer person. They are a Fellow of the Institute of Mental Health and are currently completing their PhD at the University of Nottingham, investigating the links between selfhood, identity and mental health in autistic people perceived as women. They are a late diagnosed autistic person who experienced serious mental illness following the birth of their first child in 2012. They are passionate about human rights with a focus on autistic people, mental health and recovery, gender and disability equality. They live with their family in the United Kingdom.

Jersey Cosantino (they/them/theirs), a former K-12 educator, is a current doctoral student in the Cultural Foundations of Education department at Syracuse University and is pursuing certificates of advanced study in women's and gender studies and disability studies. Jersey's scholarship resides at the intersections of Mad Studies and Trans Studies and, utilizing disability and transformative justice frameworks, their research seeks to center the voices and experiences of transgender and gender non-conforming students with mental disabilities in K-12 academic settings. Jersey identifies as trans and non-binary and is white with class, citizenship, and able-bodied privilege. They are also a co-facilitator for SU's Intergroup Dialogue Program and hold a master's in education and a graduate certificate in mindfulness studies.

Dr. Benjamin Habib is a Senior Lecturer in Politics and International Relations at La Trobe University, Melbourne, Australia. Ben is an internationally published scholar with a current research interest in Korean Peninsula security, environmental movements and international climate politics, and undergraduate teaching pedagogy. He has also written and talked extensively about his experience with madness and neurodiversity. Ben teaches into the Permaculture Design Course, (PDC) a CE-RES Community Environment Park in Melbourne, focusing on the application of permaculture design principles to community regeneration and socio-economic systems. Ben completed his PhD candidature at Flinders University in Adelaide, Australia in 2011, after graduating with a B. Arts (Hons) from Flinders University and a B. Arts from the University of South Australia. He has also studied at Keimyung University in Daegu, South Korea.

Leah Heilig, PhD, is an Assistant Professor of Writing and Rhetoric at the University of Rhode Island who identifies as Bipolar with a capital B. She specializes in technical communication and accessibility, and her current research focuses on Mad design methodologies that challenge the naturalization of "design thinking." Her work can be found in *Business and Professional Communication Quarterly, Technical Communication Quarterly, Communication Design Quarterly, Journal of Veterans Studies, Rhetoric of Health and Medicine,* and *The Sweetland Dig-*

ital Rhetoric Collaborative. She has a tattoo on her middle finger as a tribute to the late and great Carrie Fisher and hates all things related to The Joker.

Bailey Kirby, MA, is a Research and Proposal Development Specialist at the University of Tennessee at Chattanooga. She too is Bipolar with a Carrie Fisher-esque tattoo on her middle finger. Her research spans technical editing, broader impacts statements, and leadership in research administration, and her writing appears in *Communication Design Quarterly*, *Intercom*, and *Technical Communication Quarterly*. Much to the irritation of both strangers and friends, she survives without drinking caffeine and has a penchant for too many em dashes.

Jacqueline Pruder St. Antoine is a mother, a mad person, a partner, a reader and writer, a sister and daughter, a mad studies and disability studies scholar, an artist and performer, a student and teacher, a lover of brussels sprouts and dinosaurs, a compulsive exerciser, a feeder of birds, a wannabe gardener, a halfway decent chocolate cake baker. She works to bring a mad studies perspective to new spaces and investigate new ways of being, doing, understanding, and representing. Jacquie aims to make her work arts-based performative in nature, accessible, and emotive.. exploring the nuances of madness, disability, and what it means to exist in an ableist, saneist, multi-verse. In addition to her writing in this volume, Jacquie created the book's cover art.

Monica Shields is recovering from decades in public school systems as a student, special education teacher and professor. She lives in Puerto Rico where she currently works with parents and community members starting schools. Monica is passionate about food sovereignty and making clean healthy food affordable and accessible. She partnered with another community member and together they are starting a food cooperative with a non-monetary economy. Monica uses her mostly-able body, white, cis-gendered privilege to teach others how intersectional oppressive paradigms are related and how to resist their assumed inevitability. She always has an avocado close by and a stray animal to feed. Monica has late onset madness; medicates daily with the ocean, kayaking, SCUBA diving and the kindness of loved ones.

Helen Silverwood is a Mad English writer with a chequered history, and a lifelong special interest in subverting all kinds of hierarchical dualisms. She is proud to identify as neurodivergent, having lived half a century as a maverick, on the frontline of a neurotypicentric world. She's deeply interested in autism, having worked in the field for several years, providing advice, support, advocacy, and training. She is presently reconceptualizing 'autism' at autismabilities.co.uk. Helen has had her poetry published in various anthologies by Forward Poetry. She earns a living empowering vulnerable adults, and writing personalized poems for special occasions at 2keepforeverpoems.co.uk. She's also an Executive Director of *Dialogica*, the creators of Autism Dialogue. She lives in England, with her lovable, though infuriating, teenage daughter, where she writes, roller-skates, codes, and cultivates wild plants.

Aubry Threlkeld is a critical psychologist and community advocate specializing in disability studies, education, sexuality, and technology. He is the Dean of the School of Education at Endicott College, and has taught at Tufts, Pace, and Harvard University. He identifies as Mad, Queer (both Genderqueer and Neuroqueer), and disabled.

Devin S. Turk (they/he pronouns) is an Autistic, transgender undergraduate student writing from Northern Virginia and Baltimore, Maryland. Their work has been featured online at the Thinking Person's Guide to Autism, as well as in print in the 2020 Jessica Kingsley Publishers anthology, *Spectrums: Autistic Transgender People in Their Own Words*. At the time of this writing, Devin is grappling with an emerging Mad identity after over half a lifetime as a psychiatric consumer. In his free time, he enjoys playing Tetris and spending time with his cat, Maxwell.

www.ingramcontent.com/pod-product-compliance
Lightning Source LLC
Chambersburg PA
CBHW061547210726

48287CB00006B/2110